DARK INTENTIONS

CHARLOTTE BYRD

BYRD BOOKS

Visit my website at www.charlotte-byrd.com

 Created with Vellum

PRAISE FOR CHARLOTTE BYRD

"BEST AUTHOR YET! Charlotte has done it again! There is a reason she is an amazing author and she continues to prove it! I was definitely not disappointed in this series!!" ★★★★★

"LOVE!!! I loved this book and the whole series!!! I just wish it didn't have to end. I am definitely a fan for life!!! ★★★★★

"Extremely captivating, sexy, steamy, intriguing, and intense!" ★★★★★

"Addictive and impossible to put down."
★★★★★

"What a magnificent story from the 1st book through book 6 it never slowed down always surprising the reader in one way or the other. Nicholas and Olive's paths crossed in a most unorthodox way and that's how their story begins it's exhilarating with that nail biting suspense that keeps you riding on the edge the whole series. You'll love it!" ★★★★★

"What is Love Worth. This is a great epic ending to this series. Nicholas and Olive have a deep connection and the mystery surrounding the deaths of the people he is accused of murdering is to be read. Olive is one strong woman with deep convictions. The twists, angst, confusion is all put together to make this worthwhile read."
★★★★★

"Fast-paced romantic suspense filled with twists and turns, danger, betrayal, and so much more."
★★★★★

"Decadent, delicious, & dangerously addictive!" - Amazon Review ★★★★★

"Titillation so masterfully woven, no reader can resist its pull. A MUST-BUY!" - Bobbi Koe, Amazon Review ★★★★★

"Captivating!" - Crystal Jones, Amazon Review
★★★★★

"Sexy, secretive, pulsating chemistry…" - Mrs. K, Amazon Reviewer ★★★★★

"Charlotte Byrd is a brilliant writer. I've read loads and I've laughed and cried. She writes a balanced book with brilliant characters. Well done!" - Amazon Review ★★★★★

"Hot, steamy, and a great storyline." - Christine Reese ★★★★★

"My oh my….Charlotte has made me a fan for life." - JJ, Amazon Reviewer ★★★★★

"Wow. Just wow. Charlotte Byrd leaves me speechless and humble… It definitely kept me on the edge of my seat. Once you pick it up, you won't put it down." - Amazon Review ★★★★★

" Intrigue, lust, and great characters...what more could you ask for?!" - Dragonfly Lady ★★★★★

WANT TO BE THE FIRST TO KNOW ABOUT MY UPCOMING SALES, NEW RELEASES AND EXCLUSIVE GIVEAWAYS?

Sign up for my newsletter: https://www.subscribepage.com/byrdVIPList

Join my Facebook Group: https://www.facebook.com/groups/276340079439433/

Bonus Points: Follow me on BookBub and Goodreads!

ABOUT CHARLOTTE BYRD

Charlotte Byrd is the bestselling author of romantic suspense novels. She has sold over 1 Million books and has been translated into five languages.

She lives near Palm Springs, California with her husband, son, a toy Australian Shepherd and a Ragdoll cat. Charlotte is addicted to books and Netflix and she loves hot weather and crystal blue water.

Write her here:

charlotte@charlotte-byrd.com

Check out her books here:

www.charlotte-byrd.com

Connect with her here:

www.facebook.com/charlottebyrdbooks

www.instagram.com/charlottebyrdbooks

www.twitter.com/byrdauthor

Want to hear about new releases, free books and get exclusive giveaways?

Sign up for my newsletter!

Sign up for my newsletter: https://www.
subscribepage.com/byrdVIPList

Join my Facebook Group: https://www.facebook.
com/groups/276340079439433/

Bonus Points: Follow me on BookBub and
Goodreads!

amazon.com/Charlotte-Byrd/e/B013MN45Q6

facebook.com/charlottebyrdbooks

bookbub.com/profile/charlotte-byrd

twitter.com/byrdauthor

instagram.com/charlottebyrdbooks

All the Lies Series

All the Lies

All the Secrets

All the Doubts

Tell me Series

Tell Me to Stop

Tell Me to Go

Tell Me to Stay

Tell Me to Run

Tell Me to Fight

Tell Me to Lie

Wedlocked Trilogy

Dangerous Engagement

Lethal Wedding

Fatal Wedding

Tangled Series

Tangled up in Ice

Tangled up in Pain

Tangled up in Lace

Tangled up in Hate

Tangled up in Love

Black Series

Black Edge
Black Rules
Black Bounds
Black Contract
Black Limit

Not into you Duet

Not into you
Still not into you

Lavish Trilogy

Lavish Lies
Lavish Betrayal
Lavish Obsession

Standalone Novels

Dressing Mr. Dalton
Debt
Offer
Unknown

DARK INTENTIONS

One debt. One secret. One night.

When I meet him at the Redemption Club, I'm not supposed to know his name and he's not supposed to know mine. But we break that rule. That's not the only one.

He gives me chills and makes my body ache. He makes my pain go away. **He's just a distraction, but I can't get enough of him.**

What I don't know yet is that he will help save my mother's life.

What I don't know yet is that **I'll owe him a debt.**

What I don't know yet is that **he is a man of many secret**s. Secrets dark enough to break us both.

For bestselling author Charlotte Byrd comes an intense romance about debts, lies and secrets and the extent to which people go for love.

I have a secret and I'll do everything in my power to keep it that way.

I've been watching her for a long time.

I've been following her.

She's lost a brother. I lost a best friend, but no one could ever know.

She's in pain, and so am I.

She deserves so much better than me. I am rotten to the core and if I take this any further, I will pull her into my darkness.

But I can't stay away. I can't stop.

What happens when she starts to uncover my lies? What happens if love isn't enough?

Dark Intentions is the first novel in the Dark Intentions series. It is a dark romance/romantic suspense about debt, lies, wealth, crime and family bonds. There is no cheating.

PROLOGUE

I have a secret. She doesn't know it yet, but I'll do everything in my power to keep it that way.

I've been watching her.

For a long time.

I saw her going to those bars.

I followed her.

I stayed in the background. I saw her meeting with the guys whose names she couldn't remember.

She's in pain, and so am I.

He was my best friend. We did everything together, but no one could know.

We had this friendship, and now that he's gone, no one will ever know.

1

JACQUELINE

My palms are sweaty. My heart is beating out of my chest. The fear I feel is very much real.

I step over the threshold and into the lounge. I shouldn't be afraid. Everything's going to be fine.

This is just a place like any other, I say to myself. But I know that I don't belong. I'm wearing four-inch stilettos and it's my first high-heeled shoe in years.

My dress hugs my curves a little too tightly. But by the way that the men sitting around the bar look at me, I can tell that they like what they see.

I can do this, I say to myself, but of course, liquid courage is going to go a long way to making that happen.

I beeline for the bar and ask the bartender for a martini. I spin around on the swivel chair and look around the room. The club is set up into different areas. There's a place to lounge near the entrance with couches and overstuffed chairs. Then there's the more formal bar area with a spot to order the drinks and to sit and chat with the bartender. For those who want some privacy, a few tall circular tables give you a chance to crowd around in an intimate way.

A cacophony of sounds rushes above my head. The light is low, romantic, but also very masculine; a lot of grays and blues, but flattering, nevertheless.

"How are you?" Someone walks up to me. He has dark hair and his suit is a bit too shiny, but nevertheless flattering. I see how his muscles press against the fabric.

Out of the corner of my eye, I spot another guy and the crestfallen expression on his face when he realizes that he has missed his shot. He turns to his friends with regret.

"Hey," the guy in front of me says to catch my attention. "I'm Damian."

"Nice to meet you, Damian." I extend my hand. That might be his real name. It might not.

That's sort of how the game is played in places like this.

"I'm Jacqueline," I say, extending my hand, suddenly keenly aware of the fact that my real name has slipped out.

That was a mistake.

"Nice to meet you, Jackie."

I cringe. I don't like the nickname and I don't like him presupposing that he can call me something I didn't say.

"What brings you to a place like this?"

"I guess a guy like you," I say, leaning on the glass bar top. "What is it that you do?"

"A little bit of everything. I'm a videographer, weddings, proms, and occasional funerals."

"People want videos of funerals?" I ask, genuinely surprised.

He shrugs. He's making stuff up. I can tell. That's what Cassandra recommended. It's better to go with a fake name and occupation.

Of course, she didn't use the word *fake*.

"This is a place where you explore a new identity," she said, in the rich soothing voice of a digital virtual assistant. "When you come here, we want you to put the rest of your life away."

Tuck it into a small box and keep it far away from here, I think to myself sarcastically.

Did Damian get the same speech? I wonder. If so and this is the best that he can come up with, I'm not really interested. No matter how good looking he is.

We chat for a little bit longer, and I finish my drink and excuse myself.

Maybe this was a bad idea. I don't even know what I'm doing here. This is for people who are bored, and rich, and tired of the lives that they're living. Of course, that sort of qualifies me except for the rich part. And the bored part. I'm neither.

I'm more like desperate and possibly, a little dysfunctional. Still, before I got here, I was intrigued, nervous, a little horrified, plenty terrified, but nevertheless, interested.

Now, it just feels like another bar with more bullshit and lies.

And I just don't know if I want that. Despite the fictions that people spew about their names, and who they are, and these other lives they lead, the conversation that we have is supposed to be genuine.

We're supposed to make a real connection on this level that is beyond superficial. Because in reality, it's not about their job or what they look like necessarily.

It's more about the spark that you feel when you're in their presence.

Someone bumps into me and I spill my drink on the floor.

"Sorry about that."

"Fine," I mumble. I'm annoyed that I now have to scramble to clean this up before someone slips.

But then a waitress in a short, black straight leg suit comes over with a rag and escorts us to a nearby empty couch.

"Please don't worry, I'll take care of everything," she says.

"The waiters here aren't dressed exactly very sexy, are they?" I say, sitting down across from this new stranger.

He leans back in his seat and looks me up and down very careful.

"That's the point, I guess," he says. "For all of us to pay attention to each other, rather than them. They're the distraction."

"And what are we?" I ask, suddenly feeling a little bit nervous at the intensity of his gaze.

"We're the main attraction," he says without missing a beat.

I take a sip of the new martini that the waitress brings and wait for this man to look away. But he doesn't. His gaze is laser-focused on me.

Suddenly, a little spark wakes up within me, a little spark that I didn't even know I had.

"What brings you here?" I ask.

"No, no, no. That's one of the rules, remember?" He shakes his head from side to side.

Cassandra's soothing robotic voice comes back to me as I sat in her glass office going over the contract.

"You are forbidden to talk about what brought you here," she said. "You are forbidden to talk about anything tragic or disturbing, and you are encouraged to make up a fantasy of who you are based on who you want to be. If you project an image of your ideal self, then you will become your ideal self."

2

JACQUELINE

"**O**kay, so tell me something about you," I say.

"Something true?" he asks, narrowing his eyes. I like this vibe. It's nothing like that other guy's.

I nod. This might be part of a game or it might not be. I don't know. "I fly around the world. I never spend more than a week in one place. I run an international company with clients everywhere."

"What kind of company?"

"I underwrite high-risk loans."

"You can't do it online?"

"Nope, I have to do it the old-fashioned way. Meet in person, evaluate the head of the company, decide whether financing will be possible."

"That sounds impressive." I nod.

"Your turn." He points to me and then there's that intense look again.

"I'd rather not," I say. "I don't think this is working out."

I can't be this person, I say to myself. I don't know what I'm doing here at *The Redemption*? Who names a club that anyway?

What kind of redemption?

Besides, I don't need redemption. I need revenge.

I make my way past small clumps of people just as the music starts to heat up and the dance floor starts to fill. Someone grabs my hand. It's him. The one whose name I don't know, who made me spill my drink.

"Dance with me," he says. I pull away, but he tries again. "Please?"

And then as if my body is acting of its own free will, I give in. I let go, and I let him lead me to the dance floor.

The music starts to pump and his hands find my waist and then pull me close to him. We grind. There's no other way to describe it. His body is intertwined with mine. I rub against him. I'm not even a great dancer, but the music sounds like a heartbeat, and we move as one. I let him carry me away. His hands make their way down my hips and then over the small of my back again.

The next song is even more sensual and intense and when he pulls me closer, I don't want to pull away. He slides down my body, pausing briefly to worship my breasts as if they are an altar.

Sweat starts to run down my back and he grabs onto my butt, holding me tightly, telling me how much he loves my body. His is strong. The heavy weight expensive fabric of his slim-cut suit outlines each muscle. Suddenly, the quietness and the demure attitude, the standoffishness is gone.

The music slows down and he presses his lips to my earlobe. I think he's about to whisper something, but he sucks on it instead. Shivers run up my spine, and I continue to grind on his leg.

He brings his fingers up to my neck and carefully runs them all the way down to my clavicle. He goes further after that, tapping just the outside of my breasts ever so gently, waiting for me to give him consent to go further.

How could I not? I need him to kiss me now. I need his lips on mine, but he hesitates.

No, that's not what it is.

He's teasing me.

He wants me to wait.

"Kiss me," I beg, but he shakes his head no.

His hands continue to make their way up and down my body, feeling every curve, every groove, every indentation. My nipples get harder, even though I feel like I'm about 120 degrees, so I reach over and grab his head and pull his chin toward mine, but he pulls away.

"Not yet," he says confidently, like there's going to be more. Suddenly, I know there will be.

We continue to dance or rather press against each other like high school kids who haven't had sex yet, and then finally, just when my legs start to burn and the balls of my feet feel like they won't be able to hold me up anymore, he pulls me close to him and puts his lips on mine.

It's a surprise, and there's a stiffness there at first, and then I let go and open my mouth and I feel his tongue with mine. I bury my hands in his thick, dark hair, and he collects mine into loose ponytails and tugs lightly, making me moan.

"Come with me," he says.

He grabs my hand, and I follow him. We walk off the dance floor, down a long corridor, and into one of the rooms.

The sheets are satin red and the walls are

wallpapered in some sort of textured gold, and red, and black fleur-de-lis. The light is low, all candlelight, originating from the four corners of the room.

I peer into the darkness as he takes off his jacket and throws it onto the plush red velvet couch in the corner.

"Have you ever been to one of these rooms before?" he asks.

"I've never been here at all." I shake my head no.

"Well, then you have a lot to experience. Call me Dante," he says.

"Like the poet?" I ask, realizing the name is making my English literature major heart flutter extra hard.

"Yeah. My mom loved Italian Renaissance." As he moves, his dark hair falls into his eyes just a little bit. I reach over, brushing it out of the way. He smiles.

"What's your safe word?" he asks.

I reach over to kiss him again.

"Tell me."

"I don't know," I whisper.

"This is your first time. You don't want to take it too far. I need a safe word. Club's rules."

Oh, yes, I'm suddenly reminded of the fact that whatever it is we have between us isn't really real.

I sit down on the edge of the bed. It's not that the spark is gone. It's that by saying his name, I was at first excited and then I realized that this is part of the story like everything else.

He's here to meet a stranger and to have a good time. That's why everyone's here, right? Including me?

Dante sits down next to me and reaches over and kisses my shoulder. He tugs on the spaghetti strap of my cocktail dress and pulls it down a little bit.

With his lips to mine, it all comes back. How we danced, how we sweated together out there.

What if we did that here? I lean over and kiss him on the mouth. His lips find mine. He kisses me back, opening my mouth wider and deeper, leaning me back on the bed. He pulls up my skirt and finds my panty line.

I spread my legs open for him, and he kisses the inside of my thighs, and I feel myself starting to get wet. Drenched.

I want him. I want him inside of me. He starts to tug on my panties and unbuttons his shirt.

I grab onto the sheets because I've never done

anything like this. Yes, I've had ex-boyfriends or rather one ex-boyfriend, but a stranger in a place like this? A one-night stand to do anything you want with? No, that I've never had.

Suddenly the door swings open, and four people barge in laughing and talking, clearly very intoxicated.

"Oh, sorry. It's occupied. It's occupied," they tell one another, each time louder and louder.

"Get the fuck out!" Dante yells, pointing to the door. "Didn't you see the red light?"

They apologize again and stumble out even more gracelessly than they stumbled in. Then he leans over me, but I shake my head no.

"What's wrong?" he asks.

"I don't know. I can't."

"Okay." He pulls away, just like that. "If you don't want to have sex with me, I'm not going to force you to," he says, mildly insulted.

"Or do you want me to just woo you again?" He smiles mischievously.

I shake my head no, but he grabs my hand and pulls me close, and with his fingers intertwined with mine, a spark returns.

3

JACQUELINE

"I have to go." I pull away from Dante.

He nods and our fingers separate. He sits down on the edge of the bed, not so much crestfallen, but a little disappointed.

I try to find my small crossbody bag with my wallet and phone, and I realize that I had dropped it somewhere and one of us had kicked it under the bed.

As I lean over, Dante reaches for me, grabbing me around my waist, and I suddenly remember how he held me out there when we danced. My heart starts to beat fast and everything within me yearns for him.

I turn around and he pulls me on top of him. My skirt prevents me from opening my legs too wide so he pushes it up to my waist and feels the smoothness of my butt, squeezing tightly.

I lean over and kiss him.

I cradle Dante's face in my hands and kiss him over and over again. I feel the sharpness of his jaw, the harshness and the straightness of his nose.

I kiss his neck and he tilts his head back, closes his eyes, and I run my fingers up and down. I start to go down his hard body, running my fingers all the way down to his belly button. Instead of a six pack, there's an eight pack, each muscle clearly defined.

He has smooth, soft olive skin almost caramel in color. He gathers my hair into a ponytail again and pulls tightly, knowing instinctively that this will ignite and excite every cell in my body.

I can't help but moan.

"You like that?" he asks.

I nod.

We don't know each other and that's why there's the rule about the safe word. You're supposed to say a word or phrase when you start to feel uncomfortable. It basically means no, that's too far.

I wait for him to ask me what mine is again, but he doesn't. He just runs his hands up and down my back as I pull down his pants and look at his big substantial bulge.

Right before I can reach for it, Dante flips me over on my back. He sits me up briefly, unzips my dress, and pulls it over my head. I'm wearing a strapless bra, but he flicks it off with one quick movement. My breasts fall before him and seem almost as surprised about what just happened as the rest of me.

Cupping one and kissing the other, he lays me back down and reaches down between my legs.

He teases me.

He kisses me right above my hip bones and then on the inside of my thighs.

And I want him to pull off my panties already and get inside but he doesn't. He takes his time and he makes me moan and then finally thrusts his fingers and I can't hold on anymore.

"No, no, no." He pulls away. "You're not getting away that easy."

"Please," I beg.

Every part of me wants him. Even just a little bit and I'm ready, ready to go over the edge.

But he likes to play games.

I can see that now.

"How do you touch yourself?" he asks.

My eyes get big. "What do you mean?" No one has ever asked me that before.

"That's what I'm asking. Do you do it when you're on your back?"

I nod.

"Oh, that's why it was such a quick thing for you. You're used to it. What if we do it some way that's not predictable?"

"Do something, do anything but I need you inside of me," I plead.

"Okay, I like that." He looks around the room. "There. Take off your panties and wait."

This makes me even more aroused than I was before. But I do as he asks. He walks over, takes off his briefs, and I finally see his beautiful cock, big and thick, smooth to the touch without a single hair.

I reach for it, but he shakes his head no.

"You don't want to give me anything I want," I say.

"That's the point." He smiles and I smile with him.

Dante kisses my neck and then reaches over my legs and spreads them wider. He pushes me, my head onto the desk, and the cool surface feels good against my hot skin. I hear the sound of latex behind me as he puts on the condom.

Before I know it, he thrusts himself into me. I grab onto the desk and I let it happen because it feels so good.

He's impaling me and my body is wrapping tightly around his, taking him further and further inside. After a few moments, we start to move just like we did on the dance floor, grinding against one another. I raise up to my elbows and he pulls on my hair as if it were the mane of a horse.

He runs his fingers down my neck, and then makes his way around my breasts, squeezing my nipples in between his index and middle finger just a little, so that it feels both good and a little painful.

He moves at a steady rate until he starts to speed up faster and faster, and then a wave, an explosion rushes through my body. Every part of me convulses and I can't help but point my toes even though they are still strapped into these awful heels.

Just as the waves slow down a bit, Dante speeds up harder and harder and I wait for him to reach his climax and then he kisses my neck sloppily and mumbles something into my shoulder.

"What was that?" I ask, trying to catch my breath.

"That was wonderful." He clears his throat. "You're so sexy."

He kisses me again and again.

4

JACQUELINE

Afterward, Dante sits on the edge of the bed. He watches me get dressed. I suddenly feel very self-conscious about my body. It's by no means perfect. No toned stomach or shoulders. I'm about thirty pounds heavier than where I'd like to be, but he still admires me as if I'm the sexiest thing he's ever seen.

"What are you doing?" I ask.

"What? I'm looking at the girl that I just had mind-blowing sex with."

"Okay, but you're making me feel uncomfortable."

"I can't look at you?"

"No." I shake my head.

"So I can fuck you but I can't look at you?"

"Yes." I nod and he laughs. "Aren't you going to get dressed?"

"Yeah, just taking my time."

He sits back against the headboard naked, except for tight black briefs and I watch the way his muscular body moves with each breath. I finally manage to slip on my dress and zip it up halfway and I feel a little bit better. This has a nice shape to it, covering all of the parts that I feel uncomfortable about. I walk over to him to zip me up all the way.

"So this is your first time here, huh?" Dante asks.

I nod.

"How was it?"

"Much better than I thought it would go."

"Good, I like that."

"Do you come here often?" I ask.

He laughs.

"Okay, I'm not asking in that way that people ask at bars when they pick you up. I mean, is this something that you do often?"

He nods. "Yes."

"Really?" I gasp.

"Judgmental much?" He furrows his brow with disapproval.

"No, I didn't mean it like that. I just ..."

34

"Why are you here?" He points his finger at me, only half joking.

My face falls, I can feel it. I swallow hard. "No, we're not going to talk about that. Rules, remember?"

He nods.

"So, how long have you been coming here?"

"Well, like I said, I travel a lot. There are a number of these clubs all around the country and abroad. It's so much more honest than trying to get a girl who's looking for a relationship to have a one-night stand with you, don't you think?"

I nod. "I'm not looking for a relationship," I clarify.

"Good, because most people here are already in committed relationships and looking to expand their horizons sexually or single."

"And which one are you?" I ask.

"Which one do you think?" He gives me a smirk.

This conversation starts to feel like it's veering off course.

"Well, it was nice to meet you." I extend my hand, clearing my throat, bringing it to an end. "I'll be going now."

"Just back to the bar or *going*, going? We can get

a few more drinks, talk, or you can meet someone else."

"No. I'm good for right now." I nod my head. "This has been quite an adventure and I need to get some rest now."

"Wore you out, huh?" he jokes and I roll my eyes, suddenly hating the real personality that he has let slip through past his Dante persona.

"Thanks for everything." He shakes my hand and I walk out.

Cassandra, one of the organizers of tonight's party, meets up with me when I get to the coat check.

"How was everything?" she asks.

She's dressed in similarly unisex black slacks, bell bottomed and covering her shoes.

She's wearing a vest underneath her matching suit jacket with a starched collar buttoned all the way to her neck. Despite this severe look, she still looks incredibly beautiful.

"It was great," I say, handing her my ticket.

"Everything to your satisfaction?" she asks, looking for my jacket.

I nod.

"I know this is your first time, Jacqueline, and I just want to make sure that you were fully satisfied, not uncomfortable or pressed in any way. Please tell me how it went and hold nothing back. I mean, I don't need the details, but just your reactions and impressions. We want this to be a very inclusive and comfortable place for all women where they can explore and have fun and play and not fear that anything bad will happen."

"Well, actually, you've achieved that perfectly. I had a good time."

"You did?" Her face lights up.

"Yeah, I danced, I met Dante, and we went to one of the red rooms in the back."

"Oh, yes. And how was your private time? Was he respectful? Unless of course, you didn't want him to be." She smiles mischievously.

"Everything was great. He was a gentleman." I smile.

"Good, that's exactly what we like to hear."

I'm about to walk away when she takes another step closer to me and says, "We've really enjoyed having you. I'm really glad you had a good time tonight. I would like to personally invite you to a masquerade party that we're having next Saturday if you're interested and available."

I nod. "Let me think about it," I say.

"Of course, I'll send you all the details over email."

I walk out of Redemption and feel… I don't know… It's hard to describe what I feel.

It was definitely better than going to a bar and having some sloppy sex with a stranger who doesn't care about where I am on the whole thing and my needs.

Dante was sexy as hell, I won't deny that and we definitely had a lot of chemistry. I look down at a small card that Cassandra handed me, black with little gold fleur-de-lis in the corners.

Masquerade Party
555-456-7890
RSVP: cassandra@theredemption.com

THERE's nothing else on the card. No name, no location. They operate in secrecy and privacy is of the utmost importance.

I walk back to my car and I smile thinking back to tonight. Dante knew what he was doing and he knew exactly how to do it. He was so smooth, romantic, powerful and yet, shy just at the right times. If it's an act, it's a really good one.

There's still snow on the ground and my feet

make a loud squishing sound when I step through the slush.

I climb into my used Toyota Corolla and start the engine and more importantly, the heat, and suddenly, tears start to stream down my face.

This wave of emotions is so strong, I just cry and cry and bury my head in the steering wheel.

It has nothing to do with what happened tonight. It's something else completely, and it's the reason I was there in the first place.

5

JACQUELINE

My twin brother died three months ago.

Every day after I received that call, I have lived in a daze. There is no morning, day, or night. There're just minutes and hours without my brother.

We grew up doing everything together. We were inseparable. We read each other's minds, and no one penetrated our circle of trust or love. When we were teenagers, he told me about the girls he dated and kissed, and I told him about the boys I liked.

Nothing was forbidden or wrong to talk about. He was my best friend for years. And then, after we graduated from college, he moved away. He got a job, traveled a lot.

We still talked almost every day but, of course, things were different.

Michael fired people for a living. It was an awful job, but he did it with care and dedication. Large companies employed his company to come in as an outside consultant and do major layoffs of many employees at a time.

As he advanced up the ranks and became an assistant manager and then a manager and then the director, I stayed behind. I got lost. He helped me get a job in a currency trading company, but it didn't last more than six months. I didn't like it.

So that's how I ended up going to graduate school for journalism. I was still looking to do something that I really cared about passionately. Everyone made fun of my career prospects, everyone except Michael.

Michael believed in me even when I didn't. He said newspapers and the old style of reporting might be dead, but there're so many online news outlets now and they constantly need stories. The truth was that I didn't know what I wanted to do. Graduate school postponed that decision and that was good enough.

And then he died.

I was supposed to graduate this semester. This

was going to be my last one. I was going to be filling out job applications and sending out resumes and cover letters this whole time and he was going to help me.

He knew what employers were looking for. He knew the language that they wanted, especially if the employee was like me, without much experience.

But when that car hit him, the world stopped spinning on its axis. I couldn't go to class, let alone fill out job applications.

I couldn't sleep.

I couldn't leave the house.

I took a leave from school. And the only thing I have now is a part-time job at a bar that his friend owns. And I have a suspicion that the only reason I still have that job is because I am Michael's sister.

When I get home, I walk carefully on my tiptoes to make sure not to wake anyone up. It's a small three bedroom 1970s ranch style home with paper-thin walls and my niece is a light sleeper despite the fact that she's a toddler.

This is where I live now and where I've lived for the last six months after I had a fight with my roommate because her boyfriend was staying over too much. It was originally her apartment and after

I complained, she kicked me out. So I moved back in with my mom.

I spent a week at Michael's apartment about a month before his death and he asked me to move in with him after I complained about our mom and Alexa.

"I know they need my help," I say, "but I can't be there all the time. Alexa wants me to take care of Sadie because she's twenty years old and she wants to party. I totally get that but I wish that she hadn't brought someone into this world that she didn't want to take care of."

Michael listened and offered to pay for a babysitter to help Alexa, but mainly to help our mom. He was always good like that, kind, loving. He was too good for this world. I said that at his funeral with tears streaming down my face and I still say that now.

There was a fire in the car and his body was so badly burned and beat up that they had to use dental records to confirm that it was him who was driving.

It was a closed casket because the accident left his body and face too mangled to display. I hate the fact that I never got to see him. A rude old man who probably should've retired years ago called me and turned my whole world upside down. He said that the records were a match and that it was my brother.

He gave me a number to give to the funeral home, urging me to get him out of the morgue quickly. Apparently, summer was coming and it was going to be a busy time for the department, lots of bodies.

If this had happened in person, I probably would've punched him in his face. But as it happened over the phone, all I could do was hang up and shake in disbelief.

6

JACQUELINE

I climb into bed and darkness comes over me. I close my eyes, but I can't shut out my thoughts. I went to the Redemption Club, but I didn't find redemption there.

Not yet.

This isn't something that I have ever done before. I was always a good girl. I had boyfriends of course, but no one that serious or long-term. I had been single for almost a year, dating casually, having one-night stands with the guys I met at bars and dating apps. No one stuck.

I wouldn't say that I was looking for anyone in particular. Not at all. More like a distraction.

That's what it was like in graduate school, at least it was for me. Those of us who weren't involved with anyone else would meet up at a bar. We'd drink, we'd try to go home with someone, but then Michael died.

After the dust settled, so to speak, my friends tried to get me out of my funk. They tried to help me forget, not about my brother, but about the pain.

I'm not sure it is possible to do that. Not so soon, but again, I craved distraction. That's why I watched so many hours of television and read so many books, anything that took me away from this pain.

When Allison first told me about Redemption, she said something in passing like, "Did you know that Dean and Melanie went there?"

I asked her more about it and I was curious, of course, not just as a journalist, but as a human being. I found it fascinating that couples and people in committed relationships would go to places like that to explore their sexualities.

We didn't mention it again until she and I got drunk one night on too many wine coolers and played *Truth or Dare*. I had asked her to tell me the one thing that she'd never told anyone and she told me that she'd gone to Redemption.

"What was it like?" I asked, excited and a little bit shocked.

"I don't know it was, liberating, you know? It was like the veil had been lifted and you didn't have to play these games that you do at a bar," she said with a sigh. "Do you like him? Do you just sort of like him? Does he like you? How far will this go? And then the ultimate game of all, will he call? Will you call? Do you even *want* him to call? Because, come on, let's be frank, most of the time the answer is no."

Allison laughed, tossing her hair from side to side.

I folded my legs underneath my butt and leaned closer to her. "Okay, tell me everything."

She licked her lips and held up her wine glass in front of her as if she were holding court. "Well, the couple I told you about, Dean and Melanie, they invited me. They sort of vouched for me to get the invitation."

"But I thought you had to be in a relationship."

"No, generally there's a whole screening process for people who are couples who are interested. But single women, they're what they call *unicorns* because, you know, very few single women want to go to a place like that."

"What about single men?" I asked.

"Many, many want to and very, very few are ever allowed. Otherwise, it'd just be a whole sausage party." She tossed her hair again and took another sip of her wine.

Allison McGivers is my friend from Dartmouth College. We were roommates for the last two years of school and we moved to the city together. And by the city, I, of course, mean New York.

But six months later, she found a guy and wanted to move out to live with him and this beautiful single life where we both took the city by storm ended in a little bit of a disillusionment when I couldn't pay my rent. She had paid two months ahead but I couldn't find a roommate that I didn't hate so I had to downsize to a studio that cost $1500 a month and wasn't worth $500.

And that's when I realized that it'd be better for me if I even rented something in Brooklyn or Jersey City and commuted because commuting, after all, wasn't too bad. But that was a huge hit to my pride.

It is hard to explain to people from other places, but somehow living in Manhattan made you feel like you were part of something bigger, at least that was what all the television shows and movies told me.

That's not to say that people elsewhere were less but I thought that my dreams had a much bigger chance of coming true if I lived in New York.

And what was this big dream? To be a writer. The only job I was able to score, even with my Ivy League degree, was a receptionist at the same media conglomerate that Allison worked in. I worked more than the standard eight hour day. I got paid barely forty grand a year, hardly enough to pay off my loans from a private university, but that was fine.

I was good with that. This job was going to lead to another one, maybe in publishing.

Of course, I never did an internship in publishing and that's required, but how the hell was I supposed to make enough space in my schedule to work for free for someone for forty hours a week for a whole summer or semester, just in hopes of landing a mediocre paying job as a copywriter, or maybe an assistant to an assistant to an assistant editor?

But that's the thing about being in your early twenties. You don't really know what's going on and just have to figure things out. So, I continued to live my life kind of in limbo until I decided to pursue my master's degree in journalism. That way I could possibly get a job doing something with writing and put my fiction on the back-burner.

"Hey, are you listening to me?" Allison snapped her fingers in front of my face, and suddenly I remembered that we were having a conversation, about what I couldn't remember. "Do you want to hear about Redemption?"

"Yes, I do. Everything," I said.

"Well, I went there, I met with this woman called Cassandra and she laid out the rules after my application was approved."

"Application?" I asked.

She nodded her head vigorously, "Yes. I think I have filled out smaller applications for college."

"Wow. What did it require?"

"Just a lot of information about who you are. It's all very confidential, but yeah, you also have to submit this video, talking about your intentions for going to Redemption. I have a feeling that they just wanted to see your face, make sure you're not a troll." She laughed and stumbled up to the counter to get more wine.

"Why didn't you tell me about this earlier?"

"Ah, because you would have told me not to go?"

"Yes, that's true." I nodded.

"Listen, you're always the sensible one doing your own thing. So, you know, I don't know where you stand on that kind of thing."

"I don't know where *there is* to stand on that kind of thing," I said with a shrug. "As they're all happy and consenting, I don't know, why does it matter what anyone thinks?"

"I don't know. I know that you talk a good game. You're all open-minded and whatever, but I know who you are, Jacqueline."

"And who am I?"

"You are Jacqueline Archer."

I nodded. "Is that supposed to mean something?"

"You're shy, you're not that outgoing, and you'd like to be in these long, boring relationships where all you talk about is what does this all mean?"

I knew that she was quite intoxicated, but the words still hurt.

Allison knew all about the men that I couldn't stand and the ones who had broken my heart, and I hated the fact that she was throwing it in my face.

"Okay. I'm sorry." She walked over. "Don't look like I just kicked your puppy. You were pretty much just getting into one relationship and then another. I wouldn't say that you are that sexually adventuresome."

"Yeah, that's true," I admitted.

"And that's why I went without telling you."

She poured herself another glass and offered me one. I wanted to say no, but I didn't want to confirm her opinion of me as being kind of straightedge.

"So what was it like?" I asked.

"Well, Dean and Melanie were the ones that brought me, so I was kind of with them. Met their friends, the ones they play with."

"Play with?"

She nodded.

"Is that what it's called?" I asked.

"I've actually met a couple there who I had previously met at one of their barbecues, if you can believe it."

"Wow." My mouth dropped open.

7

JACQUELINE

D ean and Melanie are as plain as white
bread. We met in Dartmouth, they
graduated a year ahead of us, and I was
never really that close to them.

But I'd see them at parties. They'd been
together for almost four years by the time they
graduated after meeting at freshmen orientation.

After college, Dean got a job on Wall Street at
an investment bank and Melanie got a very
prestigious internship at an art gallery in Soho. A
year later, they held their three hundred person
wedding and bought a house in Greenwich,
Connecticut, where schools are good and the
commute isn't too bad into Manhattan.

"The last I heard from Melanie was that they

had two kids and besides being a stay-at-home mom, she had opened a Pilates studio," I said.

"Something tells me that this story will probably be a little bit more memorable." Allison laughed.

"So did you reach out to them?"

"I've been in touch with Melanie for a while and she told me. I remember her mentioning that they were doing something like this back in college, you know, swapping partners. When we met up for lunch, I just sort of asked her about it again and she told me. She was very frank."

"What about their friends from the barbecue?"

"I saw them again at Redemption," she said, her eyes twinkling. "Then I slept with the husband. Actually, both husbands."

"What about Dean and Melanie?"

"Um, I was a little bit apprehensive about that, given our friendship, so I told her straight up that I just wanted to feel the room out when I got there, but not to get their feelings hurt if I didn't want to hook up. It is my first time and all and I've never even kissed a girl."

The following morning, I called Allison again who was very hungover and sorry about oversharing. I guess, in the light of day with a sober mind, she was no longer that sure that it was such a good idea to tell a friend of hers about her private life.

When I brought it up again, she brushed me off and I figured the conversation was over.

Still, I was interested.

I was in between relationships, dating, meeting people, not really looking for anyone in particular, but still looking to meet someone. I went on these dates, I was bored by most in the first ten minutes, but there was no escaping.

I mean, I did manage to leave early a few times when the conversation became very unbearable. Sometimes, I would just go home and wonder about the stupidity of it all, because what I was really doing was going out there wanting to hook-up with someone, but I was pretending that it was something else.

I was pretending that this guy was going to be someone significant or someone whose name I would even remember. Neither of those things turned out to be true.

Still, I didn't dare ask her about the club again until she came over for the third time to try to get me out of my depression after Michael was killed.

"Come on," she said. "Come with me. We'll go

to Lemons, meet some guys, have some drinks, have some laughs."

I finally caved. The guys were nice enough, mildly interesting, but my head wasn't in it, but I'd be lying if I didn't say that I wanted to get laid.

"Tell me about Redemption again," I asked, as we sat in the back of the bar right before last call.

Her eyes lit up. She wasn't inebriated but not sober either, and I figured this might be a good time to inquire.

"What if I wanted to go?" I asked. "How would I do that?"

"Well, I can reach out to Dean and Melanie, or you can come with me."

"Okay, don't take this the wrong way," I said, "but what if I just want to go by myself? You know, I want it to feel like a regular bar, picking up someone, having a good time, then leaving."

She nodded her head. "Yeah, I get it."

"So what would I do? How would it happen?" I asked.

"Well, after I make the introduction, I suggest that you go tell them that you'd like to go as a single woman. They'll send you this application, you fill it out, make the video, and wait for a gold envelope to arrive."

"A gold envelope?"

"Yeah, it's all gold. Nothing on the front and somebody is going to hand deliver it, just to you."

"Like a courier?" I asked.

She nodded. "You'll have the date and time of the next party or event, and I guess you just go there."

"So this is just parties, or is it like a club or a bar that's open whenever?"

"When they bring in new people, they have special parties just for that. But after, if everything goes well and you'd like to come back and they want you there, then you tell them. They'll tell you the hours that they're open."

"Okay." I nodded. "That sounds good."

Suddenly my hands got clammy and my heart started to beat out of my chest. This is the first sign of life that I've experienced in two months and I want the feeling to stay with me.

"Can I ask you something?" Allison reached over and put her hand on mine. Her hands were cold, and I jerked away because they reminded me of the way that she'd held my hand at Michael's funeral. "I think you're only doing this because he's gone."

I nodded. "So what?"

"Well, I just wonder if maybe you should see a therapist, or go to meditation, or do something healthier."

"You mean having anonymous sex with strangers is not the healthiest thing I can do for my mental state?" I asked sarcastically.

She tilted her head with a look of concern.

"Yes, okay," I finally said. "I probably wouldn't be doing this if that ... hadn't happened."

I couldn't exactly bring myself to say the word *died* out loud.

"But the thing is that this is the first thing that has made me feel excited again about life, you know what I mean?" She shook her head no.

"It's maybe stupid and irresponsible, but it's no less responsible than going to bars and just trying to find someone to spend the night with. The last guy I talked to told me flat-out that he was looking for a relationship and I smiled and told him that I was looking for one, too, just because he was hot and he was a good dancer, and I wanted to feel something other than all of this hate, and disappointment, and anger that was just going inside of me all the time."

"What happened?" she asked.

"I went home with him. He wasn't as good at sex as he was at dancing. A little too eager, too quick, didn't really care about where I was in the whole thing. But, whatever, that's the thing. I went home unsatisfied and I'm sick of it. I had to lie to him about my intentions. And for what? I think I need to go to a place like this where everyone is just in there for one thing and just hope that they're really into it and they're good at what they do."

"Oh, you have no idea." Allison's eyebrows shot up. "I don't want to raise your expectations, but people there take sex very seriously and they do not like to disappoint."

I smiled and she smiled, and then we both cracked up laughing.

8

JACQUELINE

Darkness is falling and the sun disappears over the horizon. The next party is tonight.

I get the official email from Cassandra. This time however, the message is not so impersonal as it was before; she writes more like a friend asking me whether I'm free to come over.

This isn't the masquerade that's on Saturday; this is just an informal get-together, a few friends having drinks at the bar. No pressure as always, she points out.

I stare at the email on my phone and wonder if I should go. When I put on my best pair of skinny black jeans, a comfortable, loose-fitting top, and a tight leather jacket that's way too thin for this cold weather, I look at myself in the standing mirror in my room and I like what I see.

I look cool, hip, just going out on the town. I hate to admit it, but Redemption was fun. I like meeting strangers who I can have this flirtation with once and then move on with my life.

It's freeing not to know their real names or what they do for a living and it's freeing to not be myself tonight. Tonight I'm not going to be Jacqueline, tonight I'm going to be Kylie. It's not my favorite name, but it's catchy and easy to remember and that's good enough.

When I arrive at the club, I head straight to the bar and look around, couples are everywhere. One guy who had his arm around a girl with long auburn hair pulls away and comes to talk to me.

He sits on the bar stool nursing his Old Fashioned. Instead of a martini, I order the same.

"Wow, I didn't know girls liked these kind of drinks."

I hate statements like that. It's a compliment peddling in stereotypes. It's like saying, *I'm not like other girls, I'm a cool girl*.

"Maybe not, but I do." I smile.

He introduces himself as Brad and I wonder if

that's his real name. We shake hands and he looks at me like I'm something to consume. That's the point, I guess, but it's a little bit too sleazy. When his girlfriend or wife turns around and waves at us, he nods for her to come over and introduces her as Christine.

Christine seems shy and a little bit uncomfortable and he mentions that it's their first time here.

"You're going to have a good time," I say and move just a little bit away from them. I've never kissed a girl and I'm not really interested in starting with Christine.

After a few minutes, I excuse myself to head to the bathroom but instead I scan the room.

Dante, where are you? I say silently to myself.

Staring at myself in the mirror, it occurs to me that I'm not so much here for someone new, but for someone old.

I exhale slowly and I curse myself because this is the complete opposite of what is supposed to be happening. I'm supposed to meet someone new, someone fun.

What am I doing instead? I'm waiting around for *him*.

I go back to the bar. I chat with two more guys

and then a girl. She's a single girl, just like me and introduces herself as Emerson. That's such a good name, I suddenly feel jealous.

Why didn't I go with something literary and exotic instead of plain old Kylie?

Emerson has thick curly, black hair and is in an attractive peasant blouse and jeans. She's not particularly dressed up and from talking to her for a few minutes I realize that she's not a stranger at all.

"How often do you come here?"

"Um, usually once a month just to blow off steam."

"And what is it like?"

"Oh, you've never been?"

"No, I was just once, so this is my second time."

"Oh, okay. Were you with a guy or more people?" Emerson asks, drinking her Bloody Mary.

She seems completely unfazed by the fact that that's a morning drink and that everyone else is wearing cocktail dresses and I admire that.

"Well, I'm a pilot, I fly around a lot. Single, so, you know, this is kind of a fun thing to do whenever I'm in different cities."

"So are these clubs everywhere?"

"Major cities, yes. LA, New York, Boston. Let's

see, Atlanta, Seattle. There must be others. Miami, I'm sure."

"So, do you meet guys in every place?"

"Well, that's what's so interesting about it. You can kind of hook-up with whoever you want. Sometimes couples, sometimes one-on-one depending on how the mood strikes."

I take another sip of my Old Fashioned and suddenly hate the way it tastes. I ask the bartender to bring me a martini.

"You don't seem very comfortable," she says.

I rub the back of my head and lean my elbow onto the bar top.

"Um, that's the thing. I'm kind of all over the place. Last time I came, I had a really good time. I met this guy."

"Who?" She leans over as her eyes light up.

"Dante."

"Oh my God. You lucked out. And you were with him one-on-one?"

I nod.

"Dante is a stud." She crosses her legs and clinks my martini glass with hers in a demonstrative manner.

"Have you been with him?"

"Yes, and he is very, very good."

"So how often does he come here?"

"Well, he travels a lot for work and I mean a lot. I've seen him once here probably every six months. If he were here last week, I wouldn't expect him to be here again for six more months."

I nod, slightly disappointed.

"I know how you feel."

"You do?"

"Yep. We got together about the fourth or fifth time that I was here and let me just tell you, if you're expecting every guy here to be as good as him, I would adjust those expectations. That's just not going to happen."

"Oh, okay." I nod, not hiding my disappointment.

"It's like, he will be what you want him to be. If you want him to be rough, he'll do that. If you want him to be a little soft, take it easy, he'll do that," Emerson continues to gush and I feel a tinge of jealousy. "And the best part is you don't have to request anything, you don't have to tell him what you want. It's like, he knows intuitively as soon as he gets with you."

"Ah," I exhale loudly. I thought that we shared a real spark but I guess that wasn't the case.

"Don't let that get you down," she says. "This

place is great, you're going to meet lots of other people."

"I know. I just, I don't know. I came here thinking that this is what I want. I want to have a good time. I want to forget what happened and here I am talking to you about the first guy I met and thinking about how I'm not going to be able to see him again for six months and I'm sorry about that."

"But just because it's not Dante doesn't mean that you're not going to meet someone amazing, okay?" Emerson says. "A lot of people here are very good and the couples, you should give them a chance. They're very giving and you know, you don't have that same pressure you do with guys one-on-one. And since you're the guest star, you can just sort of lie there and let it happen if you want. If that's your thing."

"The thing is I don't even know what my thing is," I say, nodding.

I finish my drink and ask for another round. Two guys approach us, as she turns around to flirt with one, she introduces me to Ross.

He's tall, broad shouldered, and looks like he works out. He has kind eyes and a short crew cut that actually frames his face well. He has a little bit of last night's stubble and I like the way that he rubs his chin when he talks.

I turn my attention to Ross and the guy who had approached me leaves without saying a word. He's halfway away from me, before I reach to apologize, so I just shrug it off.

Ross and Emerson flirt a lot. They bring me in on the conversation and then suddenly, Emerson glides her hand over my arm and pulls me closer to Ross who reaches down and gives me a kiss.

It feels nice, romantic but also a little bit forced on my part. I kiss him back but the tension and the feeling isn't there.

I guess he senses that as well because he turns his attention almost exclusively to Emerson who reciprocates his every advance.

"Do you want to join us?" she asks, grabbing my hand again and standing up. "We're going to head to one of the rooms in the back."

"Um, no thanks. I'm just going to stay here for a little bit." I nod.

She smiles and nods then says, "Let me give you my card just in case you want to get in touch and get some coffee sometime, okay? And talk."

I nod. "Thanks."

I slip her card into my purse and watch her walk

away with Ross, their arms draped around each other's backs and suddenly, I feel incredibly lonely.

IT'S NOT SUPPOSED to be like this.

When I came here, I thought that everything was going to be amazing and I was going to have a good time again.

What I did not know was that I was actually just looking forward to being with *Dante*.

Oh, I feel so stupid, and like such a loser. I came here with every intention of doing the opposite of that; of meeting people, just for one thing, no strings attached.

And then here I am walking around comparing every single man I meet to the one that blew me off my feet.

Cassandra meets up with me when she sees me at the coat check and hands me my jacket. "Is everything okay?"

"Yeah. I'm just not feeling up to it today."

"Okay. Well, I hope that no one made you feel uncomfortable."

"No, actually I met a really nice girl, Emerson, but I just, I'm not ready to be with a girl," I say in a half whisper, "and I'm just not in the right head space."

"Yes, of course. We want you to be as comfortable as possible. This is totally normal."

I nod, putting on my jacket.

"Will we see you at the masquerade ball," she asks, "this Saturday?"

"I'm going to think about it. Is there something that I have to wear?"

"Well, of course, feel free to dress however you like."

"Is it like a Halloween party?" I ask.

"No, just formal attire and a Venetian mask should do."

"Okay. Thanks. I'll think about it."

I go out to my car and as soon as I get in, I burst into tears.

"Stop. Stop crying," I keep saying to myself out loud. "This is nuts. You wanted to be there. Why are you making this so complicated?"

I turn on the music really loud and let Gwen Stefani take me away to a less angry place. After a few minutes, my tears dry and I drive to Lemons, my favorite bar, hoping to see Allison there.

Sure enough, I find her in the corner with Danny Morenko, her latest romantic interest. It's been two weeks and they are still at the height of their honeymoon.

She waves me over, and we talk about work and life, and I have a few more drinks and a basket of curly fries, and try to forget about everything that happened.

9

JACQUELINE

When I get home and start to tiptoe through the house, I spot the light on in the kitchen. I find Mom sitting there, her hair hanging loosely around her head, her gray roots coming showing up in thick clumps around the crown of her head.

"Hey, what are you doing up?" I ask, putting my purse on the table. She immediately gives me a little bit of side-eye and I move to the chair.

I look over to our ancient refrigerator, which breaks at least once every year or so that we keep planning on replacing without actually making the commitment to do so.

"Couldn't sleep," Mom says.

My mom is dressed in her favorite plush

bathrobe and her royal blue silk pajamas are slightly visible underneath. They were this year's Christmas gift from Michael and she practically lives in them.

My mom is in her sixties and incredibly stylish. When things were going well, she never missed an appointment at the salon or the manicurist.

She's always been good with her hands and crafty and that's why the house looks as good as it can look given its age and state of deterioration.

"How was everything?" she asks, pulling herself away from her Kindle for a moment.

She has always been an avid reader, but ever since she got sick and hasn't been able to get much exercise due to chemotherapy and a lack of energy, she has become what I lovingly call a *rabid* reader. She devours a book, sometimes two, three a day. It's her primary source of entertainment.

"How are you feeling?" I ask.

She shrugs, pulls out a little clear lip gloss tube from her pocket, and lines her lips.

"So-so today. I went on a walk trying to get those 5,000 steps, but only managed to do 3,000."

"Well, that's great. I mean, any little bit helps."

"Yeah. It's just pathetic, you know? I used to be so mobile, so active."

"Yeah, I know. Well, listen, I'm proud of what

you're doing and how far you're getting, given the circumstances."

We are both dancing around her diagnosis, not really mentioning it on purpose. She has had chronic illness issues for a long time. That's part of the reason why it was so important for her to stay fit and active. Many years ago, before we moved to this house, we lived in another one a few miles away and my mom would constantly get sick there.

No one knew why, but she would just have these spells where she couldn't get up, she couldn't do anything, she'd cough, she'd be sick for weeks.

She went to see a lot of doctors and someone had mentioned an autoimmune disease was a possibility, but she felt still there was something else going on.

When my dad lost twenty grand gambling in Atlantic City and we got evicted, we moved in with a friend of theirs, into their small guest house and suddenly, my mom felt infinitely better.

It was a big mystery until she looked into it more and discovered that she had a very bad allergy to mold. The other house we'd lived in had a huge mold problem, but it was right behind the walls, so none of it was visible except for in the basement.

Things had improved a lot since then, but that's

what taught her to always take care of her health and prioritize it over almost anything else.

"So, tell me about Allison," Mom says, standing up and peering into the fridge, offering to make something.

At first, I say no, but then the thought of some fried eggs and toast draws me in.

"Nothing new, hung out with her new boyfriend or whatever their official status is."

"Sounds good. How's her job?"

"Very busy, working crazy hours like always."

"Well, I'm glad that you went out, had some fun. You know, it's important to have fun at your age."

There's more veiled language there.

I know that she's concerned about me and "the choices" that I'm making.

"I'm going to make you eggs in a basket. Remember? Michael's favorite."

I smile at the corner of my lips. The thing that's the hardest about losing him is that there are memories of him everywhere.

On one hand, I want to remember, and I want to hold him with me and keep him safe.

But on the other hand, I'm afraid. There's this

pain that comes with remembering him and talking about him and it cuts me to the core.

Sometimes it's easier to just not think about him and to not let that pain in.

"I got the acceptance packet for the experimental treatment," Mom announces as she flips the eggs and the toast over with the spatula.

"What?" I gasp. "Wait, you did?"

We've been waiting for these documents to arrive for months, and for her to just announce it so nonchalantly, it takes me aback.

"Listen, it's not a good idea."

"What? No, this is the only thing that's going to work."

She shakes her head. "I've thought about it. It's just going to be too much of a burden."

"What are you talking about? Where are they?"

I leave the kitchen and walk around the dining room. When I don't find them there, I head to the console table behind the couch where we usually pile up all sorts of envelopes and papers, which I keep meaning to get to.

Searching through everything, I find nothing. When I get back to the kitchen, my food is plated and she's holding a big thick envelope in her hand.

"I'm going to show you this, but I want you to put it in perspective, Jacqueline."

"What are you talking about?"

"The costs. I want you to consider the costs of all of this."

My face falls. It was such a long shot for the doctor at the Mayo Clinic to even take on my mom as a patient for her breast cancer diagnosis. But I hadn't considered how much it would even cost or how we would pay for it.

I grab the folder from her, rip into it, and scroll past the congratulations and all that welcome stuff to about the tenth page where they mention the costs.

"$250,000," I say, looking up at her, "a quarter of a million."

She nods.

"Are they insane?"

"There's a surgery involved and as you know, the cancer has spread somewhat."

"But you already had chemotherapy and radiation and all that stuff."

"Yes, exactly. And if you remember, I already owe about $150,000 in bills for all of that treatment."

"Okay, so we pay for it and that's it. What's there to think about?"

"Pay for it with what money, Jacqueline?" Mom asks, crossing her hands.

I feel like she's talking to me like one of her third grade students.

"I don't know, we put it on the credit cards like we did with the rest."

"The rest of the treatments were pay as you go. I took out some additional Medical credit cards. We maxed out all the others. We took a loan against the house."

I nod. I know all of this.

Suddenly I feel incredibly guilty for the fact that I don't have a good paying job to help pay for all of these expenses.

"Look, I'm not saying any of this to make you feel bad. This isn't your burden."

"Of course it is, you're my mother."

"All I'm saying is that we're pretty tapped out for all the medical bills that I have already paid, okay? And Michael's funeral, that set us back a good $10,000, so I just don't think this is in the cards for me."

"So what are you going to do, just give up?"

"I can do more chemotherapy or radiation here, but ..."

"No, if the Mayo Clinic and the doctors there think that you have a chance ..."

"Everything's experimental, okay? There are no guarantees."

"I'm not just going to stand here and watch you die, Mom."

"I don't think you have a choice. Eat your food," she says and walks out, slamming the door to her room shut.

I melt into the chair and I pick up the fork and stare at the food before me, trying to figure out what I'm going to do.

10

JACQUELINE

I can't sleep all night. I toss and turn and I try to figure out a way out of this mess. I take the packet to my room with me, read it over and over again looking for loopholes or options. They mention that they have their own financing, but financing requires credit reports, and both mine and Mom's are pretty much tapped out.

I could get a job, but I'd be lucky to find something that pays $40,000 a year, and that's not going to get us any closer to paying off this quarter of a million dollar bill.

And the thing is that the paperwork here is convoluted as well, so they're dealing with terminally or almost terminally ill patients who will probably not be successful and will probably then not be able to pay the bill. Somebody else has to be the co-signer, and the majority of the money is paid upfront.

I go online and check my credit limits on all my cards. I can probably get another one. Everything is almost tapped out because I had been helping my mom pay down her other medical bills.

If she or I declare bankruptcy, these other bills will go away, but so will the credit cards for more money that can be borrowed.

I'm stuck.

I don't want to admit it, but she's right. We can't pay for this, and if we don't pay for this, then the chances of her living another six months are pretty grim.

I get up and pace around the room. My legs feel tense but weak, and I slip on a pair of yoga pants and my lightest jacket and go for a run, mostly to get out of the claustrophobic atmosphere.

I run down my street and around the corner past the diner that's just opening up for all those older people in the neighborhood who like to get their fresh bread and coffee at 5:00 a.m.

This area still has a little bit of old New York to

it. There's no suburban sprawl. The houses are small and at least thirty years old, and there's still a sense of community.

There's a deli, a diner, a bar, and a pompom-and-pop grocery store, and a few clothing stores. There are a lot of elderly people who live here, because they can still take the bus or walk to get their groceries and their medications at the local pharmacy.

I run past the bakery, and the smell of fresh bread knocks me back for a moment. I feel around in my jacket and notice that I have brought my wallet.

I'll make a stop here on the way back, but for now I'll just continue to run. I run fast.

I'm not a very good runner, and my side quickly begins to ache. I'm probably breathing all wrong, but my legs still feel good. I like the gust of wind that knocks itself into me, and I like watching my breath make little puffs all around me as I exhale.

Finally, when my lungs feel like they're on fire, I stop, fold in half, and try to catch my breath.

What am I going to do?

Where am I going to get a quarter of a million dollars? I ask myself, shaking my head.

I mean, that's the kind of money that ... Who the hell even has that kind of money?

I try to think of everyone I know. Allison is at the top of the list. The most that I could probably borrow from her is $10,000, but it would be from her credit line and she'd need it back at a high interest rate, mostly because she has a tendency to forget to make payments, and her credit is shot.

If not Allison, then who? I run names in my head as if I'm going through a Rolodex one after the other.

Unfortunately, when you're poor, you happen to only know other poor people, and even if I were to meet a rich person, what would I do? Ask them if I can borrow this money just out of the blue?

What about charities? I say to myself. There are charities that help people. Well, unfortunately as a journalist, I've reported on some for school projects and I discovered that charities have a lot of overhead to pay their employees, however meagerly, so that seems like an unlikely option.

The few medical charities that I have heard about and read about will do things like pay for hospice care and a nurse just in the last months of someone's life, not invest a quarter of a million dollars into an experimental treatment that may or may not work.

I run back home and on the way, stop at the bakery. I buy two loaves of French bread along with some muffins and a bag of bagels. Food has always been the place I turn to when I am in pain.

When Dad was gambling, we lost all of our money and a moving truck came to repossess our furniture.

When Michael died.

Almost every time I've had any sort of breakup.

Unlike my mom, I don't turn to exercise naturally.

I'm more self-destructive than that.

That probably explains why I've been going to Redemption.

When I get back home, I put the baked goods on the dining table and make myself a strong cup of coffee.

I've slept maybe two hours the whole night, and whatever energy jolt I experienced earlier has all but disappeared. Now, I feel like I'm completely drained.

"Oh, wow. Look at all this," Mom says, coming into the kitchen, waking me up.

I raise my head up and feel a strong crick in my

neck that suddenly spasms. It's a few hours later because the sun is now streaming in through the window, and I realize that I must have fallen asleep on my arms right here while I was waiting for the coffee to heat up.

"When did you get all this?"

"Oh, I went on a run earlier. Stopped by the bakery."

I move my neck from side to side, trying to work out the pain, but it just gets worse.

A moment later, my neck has completely stiffened and I have to move my whole body around just to turn and look behind me.

"Come here." She points and sets me down in the chair and begins to rub my neck gently.

After a few minutes, the spasm relaxes.

Her massage gets more intense and my neck starts to feel infinitely better.

"Thanks for getting all of this, but you know how I am with white flour. It's not good for me," she says sweetly.

I nod.

She's wearing the same robe and the silk pajamas from last night, along with some sort of mask on her face that's blue in color and yogurt-like in consistency.

Suddenly, I want to cry. She has always been so good about taking care of herself, making sure that she drinks enough water and she eats only healthy food, and that's why her face looks like she is at least fifteen years younger than she is without any fillers or Botox.

And yet she's the one who is sick.

She's the one that has been sick for as long as I can remember.

First, it was the chronic disease, the mold, and then the cancer diagnosis. It went into remission and then was back again, back in remission, and now it's more aggressive than ever.

"You have to get this treatment," I say. "I don't care if I have to rob a bank, but we're going to do this."

She's surprised by my tenacity and the determination in my face.

"Okay," she says after a brief pause.

"I'm going to figure it out, and I'll tell you what happens, but you fill out this paperwork and you tell them that we have the money and that we're going through with it as soon as possible."

She reaches over, grabs me, wrapping her arms tightly around my shoulders.

Suddenly she begins to sob.

I think she needed this. I think she needed for me to step up to the plate and not always be her child, but to take action for once.

I hold her as tears roll down my cheeks, and we both sob and I try to figure out how the hell I'm going to make this happen.

11

JACQUELINE

I can't believe that this is actually happening. I put my head on the steering wheel resting briefly. When the light turns green, I continue to stare straight ahead even when the asshole behind me leans into his horn.

"I'm going. I'm going, okay?" I roll down the window to gesture to him but he already drives around my used Toyota Corolla with a dented front side and flips me off.

I don't care. I'm upset, not about him, but something else. I can't believe this is happening.

I press on the accelerator and drive and get onto the first exit going onto the highway. I do this sometimes to clear my head.

I drive nowhere, in particular, just to be alone with my thoughts.

I turn on the radio going through the channels and nothing strikes and keeps my interest. When I pass a few exits, I flip on my phone and start to blast 90s, No Doubt.

This is the music that I grew up with and this is what I listened to long after it was no longer popular. I thrash around and sing along at the top of my lungs. And then I put on Aerosmith's "Cryin'", also from the 90s, and then some earlier stuff from the 70s.

I feel a little bit better, a bit more empowered, but the cracks quickly begin to show when I pull off the exit and head into a gas station for snacks.

I'm just wasting time. I'm just trying to make sense of something that makes no sense at all before I have to go back home and deal with life there.

How did this happen?

How did my life get so fucked up so quickly?

I grab a pack of M&M's and a bottle of water and get back in my car, into my fortress of solitude. This is where the world isn't loud and obnoxious, but quiet. This car is over six years old and I'm its third or fourth owner but it's all mine, with the loan paid off and everything, which means that I'm not likely to lose it unless someone crashes into me.

I pop a chocolate into my mouth, letting it settle on my tongue, allowing the sugar to melt slowly, not usually something I have much patience for. I feel just a little bit better and I guess that's kind of the point of guilty pleasures like this. It takes your mind away, off of everything I should be thinking about or maybe have thought about too much.

I glance over at myself in the mirror, just a little bit of eyeliner and brow liner to make my over-plucked eyebrows not look so haggard. My hair has been seriously starting to get curly and frizzy over the last couple of years and now I have to rely on the flat iron more than I want to just look decent.

Why does this kind of stuff keep happening? Everything was so good for so long. Why did that have to change?

Later today, I meet up with Allison, completely distraught. I insist that she see me for lunch, even though she has a meeting right at 1:00. She manages to squeeze me in, and that's why we've been friends for so long.

I tell her what's going on, and she puts her hand around me and sits down on my side of the booth. The waitress comes over with our drink order.

"I don't think I want to eat anything," I announce.

The waitress looks mildly annoyed.

"We'll both have the salmon and the salads." Allison takes charge.

"I'm just not sure how this is going to work out," I say. "I don't know what I can do, but I can't lose her."

"You're not going to," she insists, but we both know that she's lying, or rather, maybe just wishfully thinking for something to be true that can't possibly be true.

"How will this even work out? How can I come up with the money?"

"I have no idea," Allison says, playing with her fork.

"Do you know anyone? Do you know anyone that I can borrow this from? Do you know anything?"

She shakes her head no.

"What about your boss?"

"I can't ask my boss."

"I know, but I was thinking maybe, with you working in marketing, I can set up a GoFundMe page and raise some money that way if you do a story on her. I mean, she was an elementary school teacher and now she has a chance to get this treatment and she can't afford it."

"I can ask around, but those kinds of stories usually are kept for little kids with cancer. You know that."

I nod. Yeah, and they're usually situations that are a lot more dire. It just feels like you need this perfect story in order to have anyone pay attention, and by perfect I mean perfectly tragic.

"That's pretty much true." She nods. "Otherwise, no one's going to care. If you set up a GoFundMe, you'll probably be able to raise some money."

"I doubt that it'd be more than $10,000," I say. "I mean, it's something, but it's not a solution. I sent back the materials today and they..."

"What do you mean, you sent back the materials?" she asks.

"That's exactly what I mean. I told them that I had the money. I told them to go ahead and we'll be there at the end of the month or whenever they give us a date. She'll be on the first flight out."

"And how are you going to pay for it? I mean, don't they expect the money to be deposited?"

"Yeah, for $75,000. They want it there before they start anything."

"And how are you going to do that? How are you going to get the money?"

"That's what I'm here for. I need to talk to you about any ideas that you could possibly have."

"Well, I don't have any."

"What if I were to set up a webcam and do that OnlyFans thing?" I ask.

She shakes her head no.

"Come on, I mean, there're a lot of webcam girls and they show their booty, their assets. They get paid."

"They don't get paid as much as you'd think, mainly because there are so many women willing to flash and show what they have on camera."

"Really?" I ask.

She nods. "They used to get paid a lot more back when doing pornography was kind of taboo, but now anyone with a cell phone and a boyfriend pretty much can shoot whatever they want, so it's all about content, developing your brand, just like pretty much any other business, and you won't be able to do it in a couple of weeks. That's not to say that you won't make some money, but it's not going to solve your problem."

I exhale loudly. I put my head down on the

table. Our food arrives, and she's back on the other side of the booth.

"I really wish that there were something I could do," Allison says, "but, really, I have no idea. You know that I don't really come from a wealthy family, and, I mean, I don't know how wealthy you have to be to have that kind of money laying around."

"Yeah, I agree," I say, lifting my head up and taking a bite of my food.

As we sit there, I chew loudly, and that's all I hear inside my head. I wish that the headache would go away and the pounding would disappear, but it doesn't.

It just gets louder.

The walls start to feel like they're closing in on me. I take a few deep breaths, exhaling extra slowly in order to calm myself down. The anxiety is building, starting to feel like a panic attack.

I'm never good enough, nothing's ever going to work out, and my mom is just going to show up there and get turned away from the one thing that she's ever asked the of world.

No, that's not going to happen. Not after I lost Michael. Too much bad stuff has already happened. Now I'm going to stand up for what's right, no matter what I have to do.

We talk the rest of lunch. We talk about her job and her boyfriend and nothing in particular, and she pays the bill and wishes me good luck.

She tells me not to worry and that something will work out, but we both know that's not true. I'm not sure how anything could work out without me putting actual effort into it, but effort into what exactly?

12

JACQUELINE

I'm completely at a loss. If I get a job, the salary won't be anywhere near enough. I mean, who the hell is going to pay me $75,000 up front?

My thoughts meander to other options. There was of course the famous show, *Breaking Bad*, where the guy was diagnosed with lung cancer and couldn't pay for the treatment or to support his family, so he started making and selling methamphetamines.

That would be good, except I'm not very good at chemistry and I have no idea how to even begin to do something like that.

But still, my thoughts continue to wander. My father was a gambler. He played blackjack and poker and he made us lose numerous apartments and cars, but there were other times when he won.

I remember how fun it was being with him when we celebrated. The most he ever won was $50,000 in one night. It was the most money I'd ever seen. When he came home, he was beaming from ear to ear, and it felt like Christmas morning.

He bought my mom a big diamond ring, and he got Michael some sort of Star Wars battleship and a big dollhouse for me.

Would this wok for me?

Could I take the little bit of money that I do have and bring it to the casino and try to win my mom's life?

I bite the inside of my cheek as I consider that option. My mom hates gambling. She always has. She blames it for the demise of their relationship and for my father's disappearance.

She always thought it was better to have one steady job than to live a life on the edge like he did for all of those years, never knowing when you're going to be up and when you're going to be down.

But the thing is that my father wasn't cut out for full-time work. He craved more. He needed the excitement of the nightlife. I was never like that when it came to gambling.

He taught me a little bit and we would play in secret with Michael when Mom was at work. We weren't supposed to tell her that he was teaching us to play because he knew she would never approve of that.

Michael was a lot like our dad.

He loved gambling for gambling's sake. He would get so excited when he had a good hand, but for me, I never really cared.

It was all logistics.

Could I win?

What are the chances and the likelihood? And if I didn't think that the risk was good, was falling in my favor, then I wouldn't play the hand.

I haven't played in years. Mom made me promise that it's something that I would never take up no matter how desperate I was for money, but what about now?

How do I save her life?

How do I come up with this money without gambling, without doing something elicit?

No, the solution is just to not tell her. This would be my secret. This would be the way that I try to make everything right.

I go back home and find the old books that my dad kept in the back of the closet. Mom wanted me to throw them away, but I never could throw away a memory of him.

I held on to them because, well, I didn't have much else. She threw away a lot of the pictures after he left in order to try to erase all the pain that he had caused her.

What she didn't realize was that she wasn't the only one in that relationship. There were also Michael and me, and we needed him to be around, even if it was just in spirit.

I read through the books while Mom took a nap in the other room. I try to remember what he taught me about the game, and then I go online and read more.

I read everything that I can find and I decide to play on my laptop just to see how it would work out. At first, I play with fictional money and I lose every single hand.

I fold.

It's poker, and after five games in a row, I feel like a fool. Then I make an account, put up fifty bucks, maybe it would work better if the stakes are more real and the money is more immediate.

I play another round.

I play one game and then another, and then

another with a computer or some unknown person on the other end. After two hours, I lose it all.

The fifty dollars is gone just like that. It's gone. I saw the cards, and I couldn't make them work. I bluffed, but no one believed me.

Maybe I don't have the same skills my father did, or maybe I didn't learn enough. It's probably a little bit of both.

What about now?

What the hell do I do now?

I close my laptop and pace around the room. Just a few hours ago, learning how to gamble, making that much money at the casino seemed like an actual plausible business, but, of course, there are lots of people with a lot more experience vying for the same thing.

No, if I can't win online with fifty bucks, I shouldn't try to play for real.

I could get better, of course. Learn the tricks, maybe even take a class, but I don't have time for that.

I owe them the money within a couple of weeks, as soon as they call to schedule Mom to come out, and what then?

What do I do then?

13

DANTE

I move my legs swiftly as I cover the ground, one heavy step after another. The rain is falling in sheets.

Seattle is not my favorite city in the world, even though it is one of the most beautiful places in the summer.

But it's not the summer. It's April, and the skies are gray, and the sun hasn't visited this part of the world in months.

Luckily, I don't live here.

I don't live anywhere.

I have a suitcase and a laptop and a tablet and a phone and a storage unit outside of Bangor, Maine, and that's it.

I live my life on the road. The world can be a

dark place, but every time it gets a little darker, I get on the plane and fly away.

Not many people survive in my position, doing what I do. They get restless.

They miss their friends and their families. And I've worked this job longer than anyone.

I like the consistency of it, despite the fact that I travel almost every week. I live out of hotel rooms and room service, and the only thing that stays the same are the gyms and the pools in those four and five-star hotels, as well as my daily or almost daily five-mile run.

No matter where I am, I wake up early and hit the pavement in order to ground myself.

I run before I get into the shower and get to work. I run before I sit in long, oversized conference rooms with floor-to-ceiling windows, looking out onto the skyscrapers and listen to pitch after pitch of why my company should invest in their risky venture.

I've skipped a couple of days of running, due to jet lag, and it shows. My muscles ache and my lungs burn, and I push through until I get back to the hotel.

After a quick shower and a breakfast of black coffee and a vegetarian omelet, I head over to the office and ride all the way up the elevator to the 30th floor.

A friendly receptionist waves me in and shows me to the head of the table. Another conference room, expansive, full of mahogany, with walls covered in textured and impressive designs, modern and sleek, and undoubtedly very expensive.

Dillard Vasko, the CEO, comes in soon after, a little bit flustered and out of control. He's nervous. He has tried to get this funding a number of times before, trying to set up an appointment with me without much success.

He's a little bit older than I am, and definitely someone who works many hours for a living. The wedding band glistens under the warm glow of the lights, but when I shake his hand, it's clammy and a little too wet.

"Thank you so much for meeting with me, Mr. Langston. I really appreciate your time."

"Yes, of course." I nod. " Should we get to it?"

"I was actually going to wait for my numbers guy to join us."

My face falls, and he registers that as disapproval.

"Okay, let's get started. I know you're a very busy man," he quickly adds.

I smile.

I'm not trying to put him through the hoops or make him work particularly hard, but people wait for these appointments for months.

My firm represents over 50,000 angel investors who trust me and a few other people in the company to make decisions about where to put their money.

To approve of the venture typically requires me to travel to the city where the company operates, looking at the expenses and the net worth, as well as a bunch of other numbers and then talking to the CEO about projections and plans for the future.

I'm here to analyze whether he's a worthy investment. Dillard Vasko knows this, and he's nervous.

He needs the money.

They all do, but I wonder if he needs it a little bit *too* much.

"Tell me about your profit-loss statement," I initiate the conversation.

Suddenly, Vasko gets very nervous again and gets on this phone to text the numbers guy, who's running late.

I have a feeling that person, the accountant, perhaps, or maybe the Chief Financial Officer, won't be employed in this position for too much longer.

"I'm sorry. I really have no idea where he is," Vasko mumbles, cracking his knuckles.

"That's okay. Why don't you just have a seat and tell me about your business, then? How's everything going?" I try a more casual approach.

"Okay, well, the microprocessors are selling well, and we're thinking of expanding into five additional markets. But that's where the financing comes in."

"And how much are you making a month?" I ask.

"About ten million."

"And how much is it costing you?"

"About fifteen. But you know, we're still setting up all of the infrastructure. We have a lot of expenses associated with the factories, and we're just expanding our marketing and advertising budget."

"Okay." I nod.

It's not the most healthy profit loss statement that I have encountered, but the thing about tech companies is that they often lose money until they don't. I'm not going to hold that particularly against him.

"And what are your plans for expansion?"

"Well, we see a lot of potential in Europe and Asia."

"Any specific countries in particular?" I ask.

"Norway, Sweden, Finland."

"Are you aware of the fact that they have at least five other large microprocessor companies that focus not only on that but on other features, as well, just in the Scandinavian countries alone?" I point out. "What are your plans to compete with that competition and to stand out against them?"

"Well, we're going to spend a lot more on advertising and marketing," Vasko says, fumbling along.

I wonder if this is the first time in a long time that he has ever actually had to convince anyone of his competence, or if he's just incredibly lazy.

I ask him a few more questions, and he stumbles over the responses to those, as well.

"You realize, of course, that just advertising is not going to be the most successful thing to do to reach the Scandinavian market? They're very proactive supporting their own businesses and protecting their own companies, even if you were to come in and give them a substantial discount. And it would have to be very substantial for them to even consider doing business with you, over a fellow Nordic country."

"No, I didn't realize that," Vasko says.

The silence in the room becomes deafening.

A few moments later, someone knocks on the door and comes in. He is uncomfortably tall and dressed in a well-tailored suit.

"Mr. Langston, this is Zach Blasse, our Chief Financial Officer." Vasko makes the introduction to the man grasping onto his iPad. "He'll provide you with all of the financial information and answer all of your questions."

"Actually, that won't be necessary," I say, standing up and shaking his hand.

"What do you mean?" Vasko asks.

"Well, I think I have a clear picture of what's going on here, and someone from my office will be in touch later. It was a pleasure to meet you."

I'm trying to make the exit as swift as possible, but Vasko won't let me. He follows me out of the conference room and over to the rows of elevators.

I press the down button and none of them swing open, saving me from furthering this conversation.

"What's going on? Are you pulling out?" Vasko asks, looking flustered.

Suddenly, the smooth hair that was previously lacquered to his head looks tossed and uneven. His face flushes red as his cheeks fill up with blood, creating a mosaic on his pale skin.

"Listen, thank you so much for meeting with me, and I'll be in touch, as I said."

I take out my phone and try to force this conversation to a close as quickly as possible.

"Dante, what is going on?" Vasko snaps.

I shoot my eyes up at him.

Who does he think he is, calling me by my first name?

"Look, your boss made promises. He said that if you come over, I would give you a presentation. Everything will be fine. The financing will be secure."

"My boss is in no position to say that. I represent thousands of angel investors, and every company that I recommend for them has to go through a rigorous approval process, which, frankly, you have not passed."

Usually, I'm not so terse or rude, but the only way to deal with rudeness is to throw it back in someone's face.

"No, that's impossible."

The elevator door finally opens, and I go inside.

"Of course it's possible," I say. "It happens every day. Do you know how few people we actually invest with?"

"But I'm not a normal applicant. I talked to Cedar and he told me that we have a deal."

"I don't care what Cedar told you." I shake my head. "The decision is up to me and you don't have a deal. Your company is barely making ends meet. You have no idea. You don't know anything about the market that you want to go into. And frankly, if you can't make your business work here, you have no business in expanding to all of these other territories."

"Look, I didn't know that he was going to be late; is that what this is about? You just can't handle if someone has an actual problem and can't make a meeting?" Vasko asks, his nostrils flaring out.

"No, this has nothing to do with that. That's why we had a meeting before your CFO even made an appearance. I asked you questions, you answered them…however, badly. You didn't know very much about your plans."

"Look," he snaps, pointing his finger in my face, when I let out a sigh I can almost see it collide with his skin. "Cedar made me a promise. I'm going to talk to him. You're going to regret doing any of this."

I shake my head no.

"Okay, let's just- ..."

"Listen, I gave you my decision," I say, broadening my shoulders, but not taking a step back.

We finally reach the ground floor and the elevator doors start to open back up again.

"I made my decision and that's it. There's nothing you can do."

"I'm going to appeal."

"There is no appeal process," I say sternly. "This is my job, okay? I go around, I visit companies who need investment, some of them need it because they want to expand and they can't go the regular banking way. Others, like yours, I suspect are losing money. They're bleeding from the inside out. And you want my investors to plug up some of those holes and put a Band-Aid on it. But what you don't realize is your company is going to be defunct in two years, if that, and my investors will be on the hook for all of that money."

"No, I am very good at what I do and I'm very good at protecting their money and that's why they continue to put their trust in me," Vasko says. His voice goes up and he's pleading now, which makes me even more solid in my decision.

"We're not investing in your business."

I take a step forward when he snaps his arm in front of me to try to prevent me from walking out.

"You better move or I'll move it for you," I threaten and wait.

It's a standoff.

His eyes peer into mine.

I look straight ahead, keeping my face completely emotionless.

A moment later, he finally caves and retreats.

14

DANTE

That was the closest that I have ever gotten to getting into an actual fistfight on my job.

You'd think that men in suits that costs thousands of dollars and watches that cost over ten would be able to keep their composure, but they're actually a lot more volatile than anyone else.

Vasko is desperate. He has reached out to Apex Financial because he had nowhere else to go.

Everything I said to him about his company is true, and I make a note in my phone to check on the status of this organization two years from now and see if they're still kicking around.

Being successful is out of the question. There's

no way that they're getting anywhere unless they get rid of that CEO promptly.

I get back to the hotel room, take off my suit and tie and quickly change into my favorite pair of sweats. This is how I unwind.

I don't wear my suit or even my dress shirts any longer than I absolutely have to. The joggers are soft, and a little bit more of a slim cut than I'd prefer and my T-shirt fits well over my tight muscles.

I've been bench pressing a lot more than usual, using heavier weights each time and it is showing.

My shoulders are getting broader. I've put on some weight, the good kind, nothing flabby around the stomach, adding girth to my biceps.

Tonight, I'm going to go to Redemption.

When I flip on the television, my mom calls.

I'm tempted to let it go to voice mail, but I know that she'll just keep calling, so I might as well chat now.

As soon as I answer, she flips onto video chat, a pet peeve of mine. I feel like you should ask for permission before you go from a phone call to video chat, but Mom is never one to follow the rules.

Mom and I have always been close. She had my brother and me late in life when her career was already established. In fact, she has gone through several.

When I answer the call, I find her sitting in front of a twelve-foot oil painting of herself from her younger days as a New York City socialite in the 60s. I guess there are still socialites in the city, but not the way that there used to be back in the day.

That was an occupation for her, going out on the town, being photographed by famous photographers, having her picture show up in *Vogue* and *Cosmopolitan* and all of the most exclusive gossip magazines.

And by that, I mean the ones that were glossy and focused entirely on the rich and fabulous, no minor celebrities allowed.

There's an enormous lattice window behind her and I know that she's sitting in her office surrounded by her books and paintings, her favorite room in the house.

The view looks out onto the grounds around her sprawling estate in Cape Cod. Her father was one of the top richest men in the 1940s and '50s making all of his money in oil. But she had a lonely childhood being raised alone with a nanny in this very same Cape Cod home.

"How are you doing, Dante?" she asks, her

phone is a little bit further away on her desk and she sits back and I can see her from the waist up.

She just turned sixty, but she could pass for maybe barely fifty. Her hair is cut short against her jawline, the same hairstyle that she has had ever since she was a child. She's wearing a long shirt dress designed by an old friend of hers, Carolina Herrera herself.

"I'm doing well."

"Where has your blasphemous job taken you this time?" she asks, a little bit exasperated.

She's annoyed by the hours that I work and by the work that I do.

The one thing that she does understand is my need to make my own money.

"I'm in Seattle, so not such a horrendous place."

"Yes, I've been there a few times. I wouldn't call that particularly stimulating."

I know that she sounds very dismissive, but I also know her well enough to know that she's actually being kind.

"How are you doing, Mother?" I ask.

"Pretty good. Had a bath this morning, talked to Lincoln."

"How's he?" I ask.

"Still married," she says, slightly annoyed.

"You know, you're going to have to get along with her."

"Yes, I guess so."

"No, for real. Marguerite is a very nice young woman."

"Lincoln could do so much better," she says condescendingly.

"Lincoln and Marguerite have been together for seven years."

"And for seven years I did not approve."

"I know, but it's a testament that they love each other and they want to be with one another."

"Still, a mother can hold out hope."

I shake my head; she's joking again but this feels a lot more severe and cold.

I do feel bad for Marguerite; she's sweet, kind, and completely incapable of surviving in my family.

Mom expects all women to fight tooth and nail. She expects them to fight for what's theirs and not try to make nice and that's exactly why she dislikes Marguerite so much.

Lincoln met her at Yale, they dated, and moved in together almost immediately.

Again, Mom did not approve. She's from an older generation where you didn't do that.

Of course, Mom has been married six or is it

seven times now? I lost track at about husband number three.

"She's just not a good fit," Mom announces. "I mean, she actually has plans to keep working as an ER doctor after they have children. I mean, how is that going to be possible?"

"Come on, don't be like that. If you say that, people assume you really think that."

"And I don't?" she says, moving closer to the camera.

I can see the outline of her flawless makeup and smell the flowery perfume, her signature scent.

"You, of all people, should know how important it is to have your own money and your own career. I mean, you did that back in the 70s when you didn't have to and inherited millions."

"Oh, come on," she waves her hands, "I was in the arts."

"Okay. So what does that mean?" I ask.

"Well, it just means that I could paint, I could write, I could read, but when I had you children, I was also there all the time."

"And Marguerite is going to be there. Besides, Lincoln is going to be a very hands-on father."

"Oh, please. Hands on fathers? What is that

anyway?" She shakes her head. "That's what nannies are for."

I exhale slowly. My mom is exhausting. She's full of contradictions and often says what she doesn't mean despite knowing better.

She was raised by a nanny, her best friend in the world, and there was a famous custody battle when her mom got back involved with her and forced her go to boarding school rather than continue living in this Cape Cod house, being taken care of by her favorite person in the world, Miss Emily.

At that time, Mom saw her mother only occasionally, maybe four or five times a year, because she spent most of her time partying and marrying men in New York City.

But she was still technically her mother and when she came home one Christmas and my mom wanted to spend the day with Miss Emily rather than her, because it was a holiday, she went into a jealous rage and vowed to separate them forever and she did.

She sent Miss Emily away. My mom was only nine years old and she never saw her again.

I want to bring this up, the contradictions, the lies of it all, and I have on many other occasions, but I'm too tired and not interested in another in-depth discussion of our family's dysfunction.

"So what about you?" Mom asks, "You seeing anyone special?"

"Nope, absolutely not."

"And why not? Don't you think it's time for you to get married?"

"Mom, you're upset with Lincoln for getting married after he was in a committed relationship with the same girl for seven years and you want *me* to get married?"

"Well, you know, it's good for men to be married. Bachelors, I don't know. It's a little suspicious. Like, why haven't you been married before?"

"Things have changed, Mom. No one is married seven times now."

"Listen, you live long enough and things happen," she snaps.

She lifts her hand up in the air and points her finger at me, scolding me as if I were a little child while her bangles make a loud clinking sound.

"Besides, it was six times," she corrects me. "One of the marriages was annulled if you remember."

"I don't, that was before my time."

"Honestly, you know nothing about your family's history," she says, shaking her head and bringing a martini to her lips.

She always has a cocktail at four in the afternoon.

Mom's life is built on routines and around six, she will go out to dinner with one or two of her friends and then maybe dancing in one of the last jazz clubs left in the area, catering just to the people of certain status on Cape Cod.

It's an invitation only kind of club. In fact, it's part of a country club, but you need a special invitation to be invited to this particular festivity.

"Well, I have another client to meet with," I lie, "so I'll be in touch in a few days."

"Okay, don't forget about your mother," she says, waving goodbye to me and puckering up her face in an exaggerated kiss.

"Bye." I wave and hang up.

I feel myself drenched in sweat.

This wasn't even that long of a conversation, but my mom always makes me feel a little bit uncomfortable.

Not good enough, not smart enough, subpar in almost every way.

I know that somewhere deep down, she loves

me, cares about me, but I wish that part of her would come to the surface a little bit more often.

Lincoln and I have talked about this numerous times and he feels almost the same way, probably a lot worse since he has Marguerite to deal with as well.

Unlike our mom, Marguerite offers him undivided attention and love with no strings attached.

And unfortunately, our mother was never like that with us.

You either had to do what she wanted to do, or you couldn't be part of her life and that was the rule ever since I was a little kid and that's why I'd spent seven years of my life in a boarding school in Maine instead of at home.

15

DANTE

When I arrive at the club, the music is already pumping. The dance floor is filled with couples and singles living life to the fullest. At least that's what it felt like the first time I came here.

This organization offered me solace. It offered me a life without the entanglements of modern romantic life.

My brother, Lincoln, had been together with his girlfriend for years. He was always that kind of guy. In high school, he dated the same girl for three years, and anyone who's ever been to high school knows that's like a century at that age.

After she broke his heart, he met a fiery yet incredibly shy redhead with freckles over almost every inch of her body. She had always been like a little sister to me.

Friendly, cute, always hanging around, Marguerite was around when all we wanted to do was relax and play video games. The freckles are probably the main reason my mom doesn't like her.

Lincoln and I have never talked about it, but Mom looks down on red heads. The ones that go to the salon, not so much, but the ones with naturally red hair really irk her.

The irony of the situation, of course, is that her family hails from Scotland, where you can't throw a stone without hitting someone with bright auburn hair.

I have been to The Redemption Club in Seattle a number of times. I usually like to get a drink, nurse it slowly in the lounge area while picking out the girl that I'd like to spend my time with.

Single men aren't particularly welcome in this environment, but on occasion they make exceptions, especially if you fit a certain physique, you have a certain look, and you're willing to pay the astronomical initiation fee.

Two girls walk past me, and they giggle and take a seat across from me on the plush, rich velvet couch.

One of them is wearing a skirt that's so short I can practically see her underwear, and she complains about how itchy the seat is to her friend. Her friend eyes me, blinking her long false eyelashes in my direction.

I take the bait.

They're pretty, friendly, probably a few years older than I am, but then again, that's kind of sexy in its own way.

"Our husbands are right over there," they say, and I watch as they grind against two girls on the dance floor.

In any other club under any other circumstances, there would be rules about this. I'd feel a little nervous flirting, approaching them.

Maybe they shouldn't be here with their husbands, I think, but who am I to judge?

But at Redemption, nothing is off limits. They're here because they're in an open relationship and they like to have fun.

"So what do you two like to do?" I ask.

"I'm a flight attendant," one says.

"And I'm an actress." The blonde extends her hand, and instead of shaking it, I kiss the back.

She smiles and giggles again.

"How long have you been coming here *with* your husbands?" I ask.

"Long enough." The flight attendant nods.

"Are they interested in joining us?" I ask.

The flight attendant shakes her head and the actress takes a sip of her martini.

"So, is that what you girls do? You come here, pick up a strange man, and take him to the back?"

"Yes, while our husbands do the same," they say, licking their lips.

I consider that for a moment. That wouldn't exactly be my cup of tea if I were married, but I'm not the one who's married to them.

"Okay. Let's go," I say, narrowing my eyes.

They're pretty and fun and look like they could be a nice romp in the sack, which is kind of exactly what I'm looking for after a stressful workday.

I take one by the hand and place the other one's arm around my waist.

The three of us walk past the dance floor, and their husbands smile with approval in our direction while kissing on two voluptuous brunettes, who have their hands on their cocks.

When I get to the back room with the women, my hands immediately start to run up and down their curves, and they each kiss me on my neck.

I can tell that they're comfortable with one another.

I haven't been in this position in a while. As the lights dim and we make our way over to the bed, my thoughts return to Jacqueline.

She doesn't know that I have been following her.

She doesn't know that it wasn't an accident that we met at Redemption back in New York.

She can never know.

I thought that if we were together once, everything would be fine.

I'd get this out of my system and I could move on with my life, but in reality, it added fuel to the fire.

Now, everything in me burns for her, and even being here in this room with these two gorgeous women. It isn't enough to take my mind away.

"I'm sorry. I can't." I pull away, suddenly realizing how pathetic I am.

They're surprised.

I'm lying on my back, and they're lying on either side of me running their fingers up and down my body.

One of them kisses me again, playing with my earlobe. "Come on, baby. Stay. You can just watch."

"Yeah, we need you," the other whispers. "We don't get to come here often. Once every three months is the only time that we can play. You don't want to ruin our evening, do you?"

"I'm sorry, but you'll have to find another guy," I say, shaking my head and sitting up.

I find my shirt on the floor, buckle my pants, and check to see if my wallet, keys, and phone are still inside.

"This has nothing to do with you. You two are gorgeous. Breathtaking. You're going to make some guy feel incredibly lucky."

I walk out the door before I can change my mind.

Even a week ago, this wouldn't have happened. I would have had a good time, enjoying myself, got a little too drunk after, and then flew off to my next work assignment without a second thought.

I like this system and this routine, just like I like all of my other routines. It gives me something comforting to look forward to, something to put me at ease.

But then I went to The Redemption Club in New York and I saw *her* there, everything changed.

It was supposed to be a visit just like any other,

and that was the last place that I thought I would find her.

I've watched her troll the bars. I watch her go home with different guys, worried that they might take advantage of her, but she was never *that* intoxicated, and she seemed to know what she was doing. She was there looking for the same thing that they were looking for.

But then when I saw her at Redemption, everything changed. The world tilted on its axis.

How did she find out about this place? Why is she here? Is it just a coincidence?

I wanted to talk to her, so I asked her to dance, and then my body took over.

Everything that I knew was the right thing to do in my head I couldn't make myself do. She has no idea about my past, and she thought that it was just a casual meeting like any other, except of course it wasn't.

As soon as I'd seen her, I knew that we had to be together, and when I touched her hand and our bodies ground against each other's on the dance floor, I knew that I had to feel her naked underneath me.

I hate this about myself.

I hate the obsessiveness, the stalker behavior, but I can't make myself stop.

I feel like a loser, someone who can't just come forward and say what they want and ask a girl out to their face, but there are rules now.

She doesn't know that Dante is my real name. We were supposed to give out a pseudonym. She also doesn't know that I know that Jacqueline is hers.

I couldn't help but tell her the truth about my job, mostly because I was lying about so much other crap. I want something in our relationship to be true.

I get back to the hotel room, get on my laptop, and start to track her again. I check her emails and then log into her iCloud account to see her texts.

My mom doesn't want to do it. She's worried about the debt, Jacqueline texts, *But I can't let her die. She has done so much for me, and she has been through so much. I just feel like such a fool for not trying to find a good paying job sooner.*

Her mother's cancer is back, and she needs an experimental procedure that costs at least $75,000 upfront with no results promised or guaranteed.

What's a good paying job going to do? It would have to be incredibly good paying to come up with 250K, Allison texts back.

What am I going to do? Are you sure that OnlyFans isn't going to work or some sort of escort service? Jacqueline texts.

My heart clenches up.

Are you sure you want to do that? I mean, that's serious, Jacq.

I'm having sex with all these stupid guys anyway. I might as well get some money out of it.

You're having sex with hot guys who are into you. That's very different from prostituting yourself to the highest bidder, since most of them are going to be old and gross and not someone you'd want to be with at all.

I have to come up with $75,000. I already wrote them back that I have it. They're expecting it within the next couple of days, otherwise she can't travel for the initial treatment.

What about the rest? Besides, it takes months if not years to develop enough clientele to build up that much of a bank roll, Allison writes. *You're not going to be able to do it so quickly. You'll get a few thousand at the most.*

What other choice do I have?

The conversation ends there, and I look at the timestamp. Fifteen minutes pass, and they don't say anything else.

I've been watching Jacqueline for some time, but I never knew this part about her life. I knew her mom had some health problems, he had mentioned that.

But this experimental treatment? This aggressive cancer? I had no idea.

I pace around the hotel room trying to figure out a way to help.

If I send her the money, then she'll know who it's from and she might not take it.

But what if it was sent somewhere else?

What if I send the money to the clinic directly?

The whole $250,000, as an anonymous sponsor?

She won't be able to find out that it's me, and the world would be a little bit of a better place.

16

JACQUELINE

I drop my mom off at the oncology appointment, and tell her that I'm going to run a few errands while she's there with the doctor.

Usually I'd have to wait in the waiting room, but it's a particularly sunny and warm day and I want to take a walk outside behind the medical center. The office building and the parking lot borders on a large ravine full of shrubs and trees, and an unofficial muddy path right behind the wall of the parking lot.

I like this place because no one is ever here, and sometimes it's nice to just go somewhere to get away from it all.

As I walk with my goal of getting at least 5,000

steps which I haven't reached in weeks, hell, let's be honest, months, I turn on my phone and make the dreaded phone call to the Danick Clinic.

I'd done something like this when I was in college.

I wrote letters and made phone calls to the Financial Aid department hoping to stumble upon someone with a heart to make an exception. It rarely worked, but I did it every semester because I heard the stories.

One of my friends or a friend of a friend would say, "I called them, told them about my situation, and actually got this additional grant, or scholarship, or financial aid option, and an extension."

I looked into it a little bit, about what it would take to become an escort, and I still can't believe that those words are going through my mind.

Unfortunately, ever since Allison and I texted two days ago, I'm no closer in finding out exactly how to do it safely, of course not legally, but in a way that wouldn't get me murdered.

As a journalist, I did an investigative assignment where I interviewed streetwalkers. Many of them suffered from drug addiction and were doing it mainly to stay high, but there were some that were a little bit more enterprising. They were saving money to start a new life. They came from bad circumstances, lots of abuse, and this was the way out.

In one case I had a long talk over coffee in a small diner with a fifteen-year-old who was sold by her mother to a pimp when she was four.

That was the only life she'd ever known, but she started reading books on her phone and she discovered that there was something else that she could do with her life.

She was saving up money and getting through the hard days without drugs all in an effort to start a new life.

Streetwalkers are of course very different from upscale escorts. I do a quick search on Google on my phone and find a few escort companies that are hiring.

Still, I hesitate.

The money isn't anywhere near enough, and to tell you the truth, I'm afraid. Who wouldn't be?

I have never been part of that life. Going to bars, picking up guys, and even meeting a stranger at Redemption is nothing like this.

This requires performance. This requires me to

be at someone else's beck and call, rather than my own.

And at most, it will be five hundred dollars, maybe a thousand, both a very long distance away from seventy-five thousand.

I take a deep breath and dial the number for the Danick Clinic. After going through almost the entire menu, I am finally put through to an operator, a real live person.

The wind dies down and I huddle next to a wall to make sure that she can hear me as clearly as possible.

"Ma'am, I'm calling to talk to someone about my mother's case," I say, trying to keep my voice steady even though I feel my eyes filling up with tears. "I'm in the process of coming up with the money. Her doctors have recommended her for it and she has been approved."

I should probably be doing this in the car, or at least in a building, but I sometimes find it easier to make unpleasant calls while on a walk or occupying myself with something else so I can take my mind off the task at hand.

"What is your account number?" the woman asks. Her voice is quick and short but not entirely discourteous. I pull a paper out of my pocket and read it slowly. It's more than twelve numbers long.

"I was just wondering if there's a grant, or maybe some sort of financial aid that I can apply for," I ask and hold my breath.

"Elizabeth Archer," she says. "Is that your mother's name?"

"Uh-huh," I mumble.

"It seems like the whole bill has already been paid," she says.

"What do you mean?" I ask after a moment of stunned silence.

"You paid the whole amount. There's no balance due. $250,000 was transferred, and we will be sending out the information about where to stay and all of the procedures very soon."

I clear my throat, still not fully understanding or trusting that I have heard what she just said.

"Wait. I'm sorry. Did you say that the *full* amount for the treatment was already paid?"

"That's what I see here."

"Uh-huh." I nod, wondering if it's some sort of glitch and I should just go ahead and pretend that I'm aware of it.

But my curiosity gets the best of me.

"Does it say *who* paid it?" I ask.

"No, it doesn't. Anonymous. But I guess it was paid by one of the feelers that you put out. You know, GoFundMe or local news. It is not that uncommon to receive these kinds of donations from wealthy individuals."

I stand here in stunned silence.

"I actually have a number of people on the line, so do you have any other questions?" she asks, rushing me off.

"No, not at all."

"Okay. Check your email and all the information will be there soon."

Before I can say goodbye, she hangs up.

I stare at my phone and a breeze picks up, tossing my hair into my field of vision.

Paid?

How could the whole amount be paid?

By whom?

My mind goes in circles.

So, it's not a computer glitch, and it was definitely done by an anonymous gift.

But the thing is that I never went to the news or set up the GoFundMe page.

I was going to do that later on today after making this call.

I put the phone in my pocket and start putting one foot slowly in front of the other.

"Someone paid her whole bill," I say out loud, trying to convince myself that this is actually true. "Someone paid her whole bill."

I PACE AROUND, staring at my phone, trying to convince myself whether I actually heard what I think I heard.

No more money owed?

Some sponsor had paid the whole bill? Why? Who would do this?

I try to think of everyone I know who has any money whatsoever, and no names come up.

I pace around, feeling nervous and suddenly consider the very real possibility that it might be a joke.

I check the phone number.

Yes, that's correct.

I call again and get the same menu. Before I get to the operator, I hang up. I don't know what to do now.

I decide to head back to the car to get my

laptop. Mom is still at the clinic, and I always have my laptop with me in my bag in the car.

I need to find out what really happened. That couldn't have been a prank, but what other possible explanation is there?

Who even knows about the situation? I grab my phone and log into their laborious and complicated system.

It reminds me of the internet from twenty years ago when they probably had the site set up and haven't changed a thing.

Finally, after clicking on the desktop version and zooming in on pages and pages of text, I find the right place to click and scroll over to the financial information dropdown menu.

I click on the first tab, and that's where I see it.

Invoice paid.

Amount due: $0.00.

I stare at the number on the screen.

Someone has paid the entire amount. My mom can get treatment.

Tears start to roll down my cheeks as this thought finally registers in my head.

"What's wrong? What happened?" Mom asks, rushing into the car, after probably seeing me crying from across the parking lot.

"Nothing. I'm so happy. What did the doctor say?" I ask.

"No news. All the signs are the same. Stable. At least things aren't getting worse."

"No. No, they're not," I say, wiping my tears. "They're getting *a lot* better."

"How so?"

"The money that we owe the Danick Clinic, it has been paid."

"What are you talking about?" She sits up, turns her body toward me, grasping on to her purse like a woman riding on the bus.

"I just called. I was going to ask for an extension or some sort of financial aid application, but the woman on the other end told me that everything has been paid."

"No. How would that even be *possible*?" she asks.

"That's what I thought, so I checked." I show her my phone and she stares at the amount.

"This must be a mistake. I don't know who would have done this."

"She said an anonymous donor who didn't want to be identified."

"We can't accept this gift."

"Of course we can. It's already done."

"Well, what if there are some strings attached?"

"It doesn't matter. Your life is worth more. Besides, the donation was anonymous. It's not like I would ever know or you would ever know who it came from."

She shakes her head in disbelief and then swallows hard, as a big lump forms in the back of her throat.

She tucks her tongue into the side of her mouth to stop the tears from rolling down her cheeks, but they do anyway.

"I can't believe this is happening."

"Me either."

I reach over and hold her, and she begins to cry.

She has always been so strong.

She doesn't show emotion much. The fact that she's shaking in my arms, like a leaf breaking free in the first storm of autumn, shows me that nothing is going to be the same after this.

17

DANTE

The following morning, I wake up early to get to my morning flight. I prefer these flights because I can start the day in a new place and the only people who usually take them are business travelers.

No families.

No kids.

Everything is easier in the morning.

I woke up extra early to get in my five-mile run, and now I suddenly feel sluggish and hungry, annoyed at everyone in line ahead of me. I don't have to take off my shoes or laptop because I have the pass, but the crowds and the early morning bleary eyes make me feel out of place and disconnected from myself.

I had a restless night's sleep.

I vowed to go back to Jacqueline, and I know I have to see her again, but how?

When I get to the gate, I take a seat next to the window and check my emails.

Nothing for work, just a personal one from Lincoln, inviting me to a party in a week's time. I don't really want to go, and I can always use work as an excuse.

I feel like I should. It might be good for me.

Besides, it'll get me back to New York, and maybe I can meet up with Jacqueline again.

Paying her mother's medical bill was a no-brainer. The only thing that made it complicated was that the clinic was a lot more thorny than I thought they would be about an anonymous donation.

They wanted my name. They wanted to know why I was suddenly paying the bill, and I've gotten a number of calls from people higher and higher up in the organization asking me questions that I have no interest in answering.

I don't know how long it will take her to find out, but I've been checking her emails and texts to see if she told her friend Allison yet and she hasn't.

My phone rings and I see Cedar's name at the top.

He doesn't usually call any time before 9:00 a.m., and I can't help but get a little bit nervous.

"What do you think you're doing?" Cedar growls, even before I say hello.

"What are you talking about?"

"Vasko, the CEO who you just met with in Seattle, why did you tell him no?"

"Because he knew nothing about his business, and his financials were all off."

"That doesn't matter."

I cock my head, not entirely sure that I heard him correctly.

"It doesn't matter?" I ask. Two women across from me lift their head away from their laptops and I lower my voice. "I'm at the airport now."

"I don't care where you are," Cedar snaps. "I got his application approved, and his financials make sense if you actually care to look at them. He told me that you walked out as soon as his CFO came in."

"Yes, I did, but-" I start to say but he cuts me off.

"That's *not* how we do business. You know that."

"Look, I have a responsibility to fifty-thousand of our angel investors to make the right decision."

"Yes, you do. You go there, you assess risks."

"And that's what I did," I insist. "And that's why I told him no."

"You don't understand," Cedar says. "You *can't* tell him no."

"People are going to lose money," I insist. "It's not a wise investment. He doesn't know anything about the markets that he wants to go into. He is clueless."

"I didn't get that sense when I talked to him."

I open my mouth to say something, but he barrels over me.

"Look, you get this done, or I can find someone else to do your job for you," he says and hangs up.

I stare at my phone, uncertain as to what just happened.

Why would Cedar suddenly get so involved?

Why would he care?

I mean, of course, he's my boss and he checks my work and he follows up, but he has always been very hands-off.

It was always clear to me that in this position, I'm the one who makes the decision about taking on certain risks, and Vasko wasn't even a close call.

I shake my head in disbelief, feeling even more annoyed and pissed off and agitated than I felt just a few minutes ago.

When they start to board my flight, I take a few deep breaths and try to calm myself down.

I'm going to get on the plane, it's going to be claustrophobic. There are going to be people right next to me, even though it's first class, and I've got to just shut it all out.

I pull out my noise canceling headphones and stick them on just as I flash my phone and allow the flight attendant to scan my ticket.

18

JACQUELINE

When I meet up with Allison, I'm beaming, smiling so wide that my face actually hurts.

"What's up?" she asks when we put in our happy hour orders. "I have to go back to work after this. I can't believe how long this project is taking them."

"What do you mean? What's going on?" I ask.

"Just trying to come up with the marketing plan that will work for the client. We have a bunch of the ads set up but of course, they're not happy with any of them. They approved one out of ten."

"Isn't that up to you? I mean, you're the one that runs all the big Facebook and Instagram ad campaigns."

"Yeah, so they should trust me. I mean, we still have to do a lot of testing so these are just the initial type of images that I came up with. But for some reason, they want them approved and they've just decided that the ones I chose weren't good enough."

When her Grey Goose vodka on the rocks arrives, she takes a big gulp. "They have no idea what they're talking about," she adds.

"I'm sorry about that," I say, still smiling.

"Why are *you* so happy?" Allison looks up at me, suddenly noticing my unusual, good mood.

We're splitting a box of French fries and she nervously eats a handful.

"Well, I have some news."

"Okay. Out with it." She tosses her hair from one shoulder to another and narrows her eyes.

"Mom's going to get the treatment," I say, leaning over the table.

"What are you talking about?"

"Yeah."

"Where did you get the money? What did you *do?*" She gasps, pointing her French manicured index finger in my face.

"I didn't *do* anything. It came from an anonymous donation. I have no idea who sent it."

"What are you *talking* about?" The tone of her voice changes, dropping an octave.

"You heard me. I called to ask for some financial aid information and they said that the bill has been paid, everything's ready to go. She's leaving in five days."

Allison leans over, propping her head up with one hand. "Oh my God, are you serious? This is going to happen?"

"Yes!" I screech.

Allison leans over the food and drinks to wrap her arms around me.

"I'm so relieved. This is going to be so good. Everything's going to be fine."

"Yeah, I think so, too," I say, choking up, trying to hold back tears.

I've already cried so much over the diagnosis, feeling nothing but hopelessness, and now that there's actually good news on the horizon, I find myself crying over the good news as well.

We have a couple of drinks, and we talk more about her work and my mom's treatment.

I tell her that I'll be traveling there with her, but most likely end up hanging out at the hospital, not doing much of anything, but just supporting her.

There's going to be a surgery and then a wait and see kind of situation.

"Listen, before you do all that, let's go to the masquerade party together," Allison suggests.

Her question takes me by surprise.

"You mean at Redemption?" I ask.

She nods. "It's this Saturday, remember?"

"Yeah, but I don't know."

"Well, you already went there by yourself, and you had a good time."

"Yeah, but when I went back, it wasn't that great."

"Okay, so the third time is the charm." She smiles. "Let's just go together. Girls' night. Maybe we'll find a couple of interesting guys and have a little fun."

"Look, I'm not going to fool around with you if that's what you're getting at," I joke.

"No, not at all. Who even says that I'm interested in *you* of all people?" Allison is quick with a retort and we crack up laughing.

Neither of us are homophobic in the least, but we're also completely inexperienced when it comes to women.

I'm not particularly interested in that, and neither is she.

But something about going *there* with her as my wing woman so to speak, piques my interest.

"I don't know. I was really thinking of not going to Redemption again."

"Oh, c'mon," she pleads. "It'll be a lot more fun than simply going to a bar and picking up some stranger. And if you don't want to do anything, you don't have to. We can just go to the lounge for a little bit, feel the room out."

I tap my fingers on the table thinking, popping another French fry into my mouth.

"Besides, you know you want to come. I mean, what if Dante shows up?" Allison says, raising an eyebrow.

My heart skips a beat.

I lick my lips.

As soon as our eyes meet again, she giggles and says, "Yeah, you'll be there."

WHEN I SENT BACK an email to Cassandra telling her that I'd be there, she replied "Yes" with a smiling emoji.

I'm tempted to ask if Dante will be there as

well. I put my fingers on the keys to try to write her about it but I can't bring myself to do it.

My nerves get the best of me as I sit with my laptop on the couch while my mom sleeps in the other room.

I know that this is going to be fun. I deserve this. There's going to be days and days of waiting in a hospital room, and then just holding my breath to see whether the treatment works, and I need something good in my life to excite me.

In the beginning, the first time that I went to Redemption, it was a way to put my brother's death behind me, but now it's something different.

It's a way to celebrate. But it's also about possibly seeing *him* again. I feel like a fool, but I need to know whether our connection was real. Not in the sense that I'm expecting it to go any further, but in the sense that I didn't just dream Dante up. I didn't just imagine this guy that swept me off my feet and showed me what real chemistry in the bedroom feels like.

Afternoon rain rolls in and I grab a blanket from the cubby in the corner and wrap myself in it. I love times like this when you have nowhere to go and nothing to do. The problem is that I've allowed the rain and all the mourning of my brother to throw me off course.

What do I do now if my mom recovers? No, *when* she recovers?

Where do I go?

What do I do?

I have to make some decisions about my life and I don't know where to start.

I pull out my Kindle, find one of my favorite authors, and start to read. I haven't been able to focus on anything, let alone fiction for a long time, but now the words sweep me away.

Two hours later when Mom wakes up and wobbles into the living room, I look up and finish reading the last page of the book that I started before Michael's death.

"I actually read this whole thing," I tell her. "I tried so many times since before ..."

My words trail off. I don't want to say his name. I don't want to mention his death or funeral out loud, but she gets the point.

"And now that was the first time I got really engrossed and just lost myself in the story."

"Good," Mom says, walking over and kissing me on the top of my head. "That's what you want. Time heals all things." And suddenly I want to cry.

"No, it doesn't mean that you're going to forget him," Mom says, shaking her head. "None of us will, but you have to live your life and you can't just be perpetually stuck in this loop of mourning and sadness."

"Yeah, I know," I mumble, swallowing back the lump in my throat that is just about to pull the tears all the way to the surface. "I'm just so happy you got this approval for the treatment, and we're going there on Monday."

"Yeah, me, too. Tell me. I know I asked you this before, but did you get yourself in trouble doing something like this?"

I shake my head no quickly.

"You can tell me."

"No, not at all. I didn't do anything. I have no idea who even gave the money."

"I'm not going to be mad at you," Mom says. "The thing is that after all that time and all those years with your father, I'm used to the deception. I know that just like him, you did it for a greater good. So was it Blackjack? Poker? Something else?"

"No, it was none of that."

"Okay, fine. Keep your secrets to yourself, but if I do get sicker and I'm on my death bed, I expect you to tell me the truth."

She's joking. This is her idea of a dark sense of humor.

"Come on, don't talk like that. The treatment's going to work."

"Let's hope so," Mom says, squeezing my cheek a little too tightly between her index finger and thumb.

"Listen, I'm going to go out tonight with Allison to a club. I'm meeting her at ten."

"Okay. I don't know how you can stay out so late, but have a good time. You deserve it. Celebrate for both of us."

I nod. "I will."

Later that evening after regretfully eating some macaroni and cheese and getting little bit too bloated as a result, I consider canceling the whole endeavor altogether.

My dress doesn't fit well. I feel like I'm retaining water, and suddenly I look like I'm twenty pounds heavier than I used to be, and I wasn't particularly thin to start with.

"I can't go." I shake my head when I call Allison at nine.

"What are you talking about, you can't go? Of course, you're going."

She turns on video chat and she rolls her eyes

when she sees my face on the other end.

"Haven't you even washed your hair?"

"Yes, I did."

"So why does it look like *that*?"

I glance at my reflection in the phone.

"Well, it dried and I didn't dry it with the blow dryer."

"Get a flat iron and fix it. It's all frizzy and curly in weird spots."

"Look, I don't need to do that because I'm not going. I've changed my mind."

"I know you're just freaking out. I know that you're this huge introvert who loves nothing better than canceling plans."

"What are you talking about?" I ask, pulling the phone away from my face and scrunching up my eyebrows.

"I read about you. There was like a whole article about it on *Apple News*. You're one of those people that, you know, loves the idea of making plans, loves the idea of going somewhere, but then flakes out. You do that all the time. Apparently, it's a whole introvert thing."

"I wouldn't know anything about it." I roll my eyes.

"I'm going to come to your house, help you get

ready, and then we're going to go to Redemption and find Dante."

"He's not even going to be there," I say, moping.

"You don't know that. This is a big party."

I shake my head.

"I'm going to be there in ten minutes. I expect you to open the door."

19

JACQUELINE

I 'm still on the fence about whether or not I want to go to this party tonight. I have a simple cocktail dress, no gown, and no mask. I looked at the Party City store, but everything looked pretty cheap and not particularly alluring, almost comical in design.

I should have ordered one online, but I had no plans of coming until recently. Still, Allison is right.

I do have a tendency to cancel on plans at the very last minute. It's like I just have this anxiety about going and I don't want to.

I always think that I will have a great time and plan on going, but when the time actually comes, I want to stay home.

It was like that the first time I went there.

It was like that the second, but going there with Allison tonight?

I don't know.

The doorbell rings and she looks stunning.

High heels, floor-length gown, hair in thick, flowing curls down her long neck.

Her makeup is flawless. Her face is contoured and the winged eyeliner around her eyes brings out their green color.

"You look amazing," I say, looking at my own sweats and my pasty complexion.

"You will look great, too. C'mon." She grabs my hand and pulls me toward my bedroom. "It'll be like the good old days."

The ceilings of the room are abnormally low and waterlogged in parts from a recent flooding. But luckily, everything in the overstuffed closet wasn't affected.

Allison looks through my clothes, pushing aside each item with great force before spotting the cocktail dress that I was thinking of wearing. "This will be perfect."

"Okay. What about the fact that everyone's going to be in gowns?"

"You can never go wrong with a short black dress. You know that."

"I'm going to be really underdressed."

"No, you're not. Besides, it's better to be underdressed than overdressed. What if everyone there is wearing short dresses like yours and I'm dressed like Miss America?"

"Yeah. It would be really embarrassing to look like Miss America." I say, my voice steeped in sarcasm.

"Sit down." She pushes me down to the floor, taking off her heels, and gets on her knees behind me.

This is the way that she would always do my hair and makeup back at Dartmouth. I was like her doll. I never liked to do it myself, and she loved to do mine.

On this occasion, just like before, she even came prepared with a little bag of her own tools, including the hairdryer and some of her favorite makeup brushes.

"Look, I don't know if I really want to go to this thing," I say, as she lines my eyes after applying foundation to my face.

"It's going to be fun." She gestures for me to pucker my lips.

"Why can't we just go to a regular club?"

"What is it that you don't like about this place?"

"I don't know. It's just stupid. I guess it's the expectation, you know? It's like everyone you meet, there's like a point to go into the back room. You can't just chat and get a number and that's it."

"I thought that's what you *liked* about it." She furrows her brows.

"I did, but ..."

"Man, this Dante guy really got in your head, didn't he?" She pulls the brush away from my face and peers into my eyes.

"No." I shake my head, but feel myself blushing.

"Yes, he did. I mean, look at how you're acting."

"I just don't think that place is for me."

I tell her to turn around so that I can put on the dress, and when I look at myself in the mirror with the way that she has styled my hair and done my makeup, I'm shocked.

I look so different and yet the same, but it's almost like different features have been highlighted.

My cheekbones are suddenly pronounced, my lips are thicker, my eyes are bigger, but yet at the same time I look thinner and more toned.

"How did you do this?" I gasp.

"Contouring goes a long way." Allison smiles, proud of her work. "So are we going to Redemption or what?"

"I don't have a mask." I shake my head.

"You're in luck. I have two."

"Of course, you do." I let out a deep sigh of exasperation. "Fine. But I'm just going to hang out in the lounge area. I don't want any pressure."

We take a ride share car over to the club and drop our coats off upfront. Cassandra's there and flashes a smile of approval.

"You ladies look beautiful tonight," she says in the smooth voice of a late night radio disc jockey. "And those masks, exquisite."

"I got them in Venice," Allison announces.

"You did?" Cassandra gushes, dressed in a floor-length, shimmery silver gown. Moving fluidly back and forth, she reminds me of a snowflake falling from the sky.

I'm again tempted to ask her about Dante, but I bite my tongue.

Allison grabs our drinks and we find a comfortable spot in the corner of the lounge area near the big purple velvet chairs. From here, we can survey the whole room, including the bar area, the entrance, and the dance floor and see if anyone interesting comes around.

Being back here makes us also a bit difficult to

approach since we aren't sitting anywhere prominent like the bar.

That's fine by me, but Allison looks frustrated.

"No one's going to talk to us here."

"Listen, I'm here. I said I would come. What more do you want?"

Allison twirls her bangles around her wrist and taps her foot on the floor.

"I wasn't going to tell you this, but I was going to try something new tonight," she says, tucking a thick curl of hair behind her ear.

"What are you talking about?" I narrow my eyes.

"I am going to kiss a girl."

"Wow." I pull my mask away from my face and lean closer to her. "What do you mean?"

"Well, I've never kissed one before, so I thought that I would here. You see all these couples and their friends. It looks… nice."

"You want to be the guest star in someone else's relationship?" I ask with a tinge of sarcasm.

She shrugs her shoulders, tilting her head from one side to another. "Yeah, maybe. What's wrong with that?"

"No, nothing. I mean, I guess everyone here likes that."

"Look, you could be a little bit *less* judgmental."

"No, I'm not. Sorry. I'm just in a bad mood. I'm not judging you at all. Obviously, I want you to have fun and do whatever you want."

"I know what's going on here." Allison narrows her eyes. "You're jealous."

"I'm jealous?" This takes me by surprise. I sit back in my chair and take a sip of my martini. "What would I be jealous of?"

"Maybe you want my first time kissing a girl to be with you. I mean, we have been friends since college. We've seen many of our roommates make out with each other at parties."

"Yeah, to impress some guys in fraternities. That's pathetic," I say, making a face.

"Of course, it's pathetic, but still. They got to experience something interesting. Haven't you ever thought about it?"

"Um, frankly, no, not really. I mean, girls are hot, sexy, curvy, but I'm not sexually attracted to them. Or to you."

"Fine," Allison says exasperated. "I'm going to go find me a date."

She lifts her hands, wrapping her thin, manicured fingers around the sides of the couch, pulling herself up to her feet.

"Boy or girl?" I yell off to her.

She flips her hair back and stares me down, and then we both crack up laughing.

Allison and I have known each other for a long time.

We met in Hanover, New Hampshire, and we were inseparable for four years.

We like to stream the same shows, we laugh at the same jokes. Still, there are parts of her that I don't understand, and of course there are parts of me that she doesn't either.

When my mom first got sick, I didn't hear from Allison for a while. I was angry, upset. I wished she would have at least texted, let alone sent me something.

I felt like I was forgotten, but then we talked about it and she apologized. She told me that she just had a hard time dealing with trauma like that.

She wanted to be there for me, but she couldn't deal with hospitals, and she didn't even want to talk to me about it.

I didn't understand.

There were months when we didn't talk, but after a while, I realized that it would be more important for me to have a friend on whatever terms and to have her in my life instead of judging her for not being there for me.

Some things are hard for some people, and I was willing to understand that.

But when Michael died, things changed.

Allison sent flowers. She wrote me a poignant card.

She cried with me at the funeral and she held my hand. She cried so much, and her tears were so heartfelt, and I felt like we were united by our grief.

I didn't realize that she would be that emotional, and my heart suddenly went out to her. She wasn't lying when she said that she couldn't deal with death.

She was telling me the truth.

I sit in the back and nurse my drink and watch the couples pair off and flirt and run their hands casually around each other's waists.

It's not just couples either; some break up into threesomes and foursomes. It's a mixture of gowns and cocktail attire, but everyone's wearing a mask. The suits look expensive, the watches even more so, and the hair and the dresses are flawless.

After a few minutes and I get a jolt of liquid courage from my martini, I start to feel a little peppier.

The last time I came here, I sat front and center available to talk to anyone. But out here in the corner as a wallflower, it feels so much more safe.

I can observe, I can be here, but I'm not bound to participate.

It's true what Allison said. For anyone to talk to me, they'd have to break away from their group, walk all the way over here to the darkness, and have something to say.

No one has done that, and hopefully no one will, and, frankly, that's perfectly fine with me.

"Jacqueline?" he says and shivers run down my spine.

20

DANTE

It's a crisp April day. The air is just turning a little bit warm, but the darkness is still hanging around.

I love coming back to New York. The trees are naked, waiting for the green buds to sprout, but the streets are busy full of life.

I have an apartment here that waits for me as my home base. I arrived early and immediately traveled to Manhattan for work.

The meeting went well. The CEO was prepared. He gave a good presentation and all of his financials seemed to be in order.

The wine starts to flow as soon as I arrive. My brother and I work a lot of hours. We don't get to spend too much time together and when we do get a little bit of one-on-one without our mom or Marguerite, I revel in it. I don't have a problem with his wife, but with three people the dynamic is a little bit different.

My brother and I were never particularly close growing up. He was a lot more into video games. I was a lot more into the stock market and sports, but as we got older, we appreciated each other a little bit more.

I'm four years older than he is and when we were kids, it felt like a lifetime. I was graduating from high school when he was just entering, and I was already in ninth grade when he was just leaving elementary school.

But after college, we took a trip to South Africa together. We went on a safari, not to shoot any animals, but to look at them, and marvel at the wild. I was going through a photography phase, and I still have some of the photographs from that trip framed in my somewhat abandoned New York apartment.

"Thanks for meeting up with me," Lincoln says, giving me a smile.

"Of course. What has it been, a month since we saw each other like this?"

"Yeah, more like two," Lincoln says.

He's dressed in his usual attire, a nicely tailored gray suit, open collar, no tie. He's tan from his propensity to play tennis, outside regardless of the weather.

We stopped competing on running miles against each other when I beat him, seven times in a row.

He's a much faster sprinter than I am, but I have endurance that can outlast him.

After quickly gobbling up an expensive glass of wine, I pour myself another, while Lincoln still nurses his.

"Actually, do you mind if we get some Jack Daniel's?" he asks.

"Yeah, of course."

Jack on the rocks is usually reserved only for a serious discussion in my family.

"What's going on?" I ask. "Something wrong with you and Marguerite?"

"No, no. Everything's great."

"Work?" He shakes his head no.

He works at an investment bank downtown and already made it to managing partner, one of the youngest.

Lincoln plays with his diamond cuff links. I gave those to him for Christmas, and I wonder whether he wore them for this particular occasion, or whether he actually likes them.

"Do you like wearing those things?" I ask, unable to keep my curiosity to myself.

"Oh, the cuff links? Of course. They're my favorite. They go with everything."

I smile, running my fingers through my hair, which is in bad need of a haircut. The strands are getting so long, they're falling into my eyes.

Lincoln looks up, makes a note of this, but says nothing.

The last time we had a big blow-up fight about nothing in particular, we made an agreement. We were not going to judge each other on things that do not truly matter, and ever since then, our relationship has been much improved.

"How's work?" I ask.

Lincoln just shrugs and turns his face away. "You know how it is, tiresome, a little boring."

"You know you don't have to be there," I say, grabbing a slice of bread and breaking it open with my hands.

I butter one side and take a big bite as we wait for the appetizers to arrive. "We have more than enough money."

"We?" Lincoln raises his eyebrow.

"I'm just saying, you know that there's a trust. You know that the work that you do can be something that you enjoy and not just something that you force yourself into."

"Listen, you and I both know about the trust and the rules of the trust."

I nod.

"Marguerite is not part of it. Listen, I think you could probably take them to court and say that ..."

"Nope, I can't. Mom pays for the summer house, I couldn't afford any of that, not even on my salary." He shakes his head.

"You don't know what it's like to just try to constantly compete with everyone around you, only it's not an even playing field."

I want to roll my eyes. We're about as privileged as a family can get. Yes, there are some strings attached to a trust that's preventing him from accessing millions of dollars, but he makes over half a million dollars a year and that doesn't include bonuses that can triple that amount.

"What? You don't agree with me?" Lincoln folds his arms across his chest, pouting.

I take another bite of the bread. "Listen, all I was saying is that you deserve to do something you enjoy for a living and it doesn't have to be what you currently do."

"Really?" He leans over, glaring into my eyes. "Do you know that she makes seventy grand as an ER doctor? Can *you* live on so little?"

"Yes," I say, "lots of people do."

"Well, I don't intend to be that person."

I take a deep breath and exhale slowly. This has always been a thing about Lincoln. He has always had a chip on his shoulder about what he has and what he doesn't in life.

Yes, we come from an incredibly wealthy family, but there are rules governing that. If you want access to that money, you have to play it by them.

Him marrying Marguerite was a big no-no. It's laid out in my grandfather's will that the only person that he is allowed to marry is someone from a family of comparable means.

The definition of comparable means is, of course, open to dispute in court, but merely taking that action would be throwing in the possibility of losing everything.

Lincoln is the kind of guy who plays things safe. After college, he got an internship at an investment bank, then a job and he started growing through the ranks.

He puts in insane hours, and I don't think that he has ever given it any consideration whether he even enjoys what he does for a living or whether he even has that right.

"Look, you act like you're above all of this but you're not." Lincoln points his finger in my face.

The glasses of wine and the Jack Daniel's are going to his head.

"I'm tired of it, you know? I'm tired of you being this I'm this guy above everything kind of persona," he says, rounding his words but not slurring them quite yet.

"I'm not like that at all."

"Yes, you are. I mean, that's why you have no relationship, that's why you have no apartment."

"I have an apartment."

"Okay, an apartment that you actually use, one you actually live in."

"Okay, so? I work and fly a lot for work," I say, slouching in my chair.

"What does that matter?" Lincoln continues to ramble. "Obviously, you're running away. You have always been running away. And don't pretend that the work that you do, meeting with all of these CEOs and analyzing risk and deciding whether you're going to give them money that they desperately need, that's not some major power trip? What makes you think that you even know what is and what isn't going to work? Yeah, you have some experience but you'd never invest in my company."

"What was that?" I ask and suddenly, the expression on his face changes.

"Nothing."

"You have a company?" I ask.

"I don't want to talk about it."

I press some more but he just clams up. He was like this as a kid as well. He'll tell me in his own time and his own time might take a while.

After our appetizers of Ahi tuna and macadamia nut cream cheese arrive, he grabs his tumbler of Jack Daniel's and I lift up my glass.

"Sorry that this started off on some kind of a tepid note," Lincoln says, "but I actually have some news to share."

"Okay." I nod.

"Marguerite is having a baby."

"Oh my God," I say, after a long pause.

"Wow, I'm so excited for you," I force the words out of my mouth even though I'm stuck more in disbelief than excitement. Luckily, he doesn't seem to notice.

We clink our glasses and he finishes his and asks

the waiter for another. He's celebrating, right? Of course he is, I say to myself.

"I'm so happy for you. How far along is she?"

"Fifteen weeks. She's been kind of sick so that's why she didn't want to meet up with Mom the few times that she invited us over."

I nod. He doesn't have to say it out loud since we both know perfectly well what Mom thinks about Marguerite.

"Look, she's going to come around. You're going to give her her first grandchild," I say.

"Yeah, not so sure about that but it will be her first grandchild, maybe her only one."

I laugh, knowing exactly what he's referring to.

"Marguerite is over the moon. She's always wanted kids," Lincoln says.

"And what about you?"

"I'm happy, of course." And yet I hear a little bit of disappointment in his voice.

"You know, it's okay if you're scared or unsure. I mean, this is a major life change."

"I'm fine. You know me, just got to put in those hours and ..."

"Well, what's going to happen when the baby comes?" I ask.

"What do you mean?"

"I mean, aren't you going to help take care of it?"

"Uh, of course, I'm the father." Lincoln rolls his eyes.

"Okay, good." I nod.

Lincoln bites the inside of his mouth, looking up at me in that way that makes me convinced of the fact that he's lying. "Marguerite will need your help, you know?"

"Look, she and I, we have a certain way of doing things. We have a division of labor."

"Okay, now," I say, "but you haven't had a child before. You can't expect her to do *everything*."

"Of course not, that's why we're going to get a nanny."

I shake my head.

"What? You don't approve of nannies now?"

"No, I'm not saying that. But you'll need to connect with this baby, otherwise, you're just going to be like ..."

"Like who?" Lincoln leans over the table trying to intimidate me. I shouldn't finish the sentence, but suddenly, I can't make myself stop.

"You know who," I say, narrowing my eyes.

"You mean like our *dad*?"

"Of course, like our dad."

"I'm not going to be anything like him," Lincoln snaps.

He rushes to his feet, slamming his knee into the table. The glasses rattle, making a loud clinking sound that makes everyone in our vicinity turn to look at us.

I ask him to sit down, but he just throws his napkin on his food and walks away.

Our entrees haven't arrived yet and I hope that he hasn't left for good. A few moments later, I see Lincoln disappear into the bathroom.

I don't want to follow him, and I'm not intending on apologizing. Of course, I shouldn't tell him what kind of father he should be since I have no intentions of ever being one myself.

Surprisingly, given our mom's propensity to marry, Lincoln and I share the same asshole, who we call dad.

He's arrogant, self-important, spoiled, life of the party, and everyone loves him. New York society worships at his feet, and if he is invited to a dinner party, you know it's going to be a good one.

Our father is the famous Archibald Tanner, a playboy, a womanizer, part owner of Playboy magazine, and a critically renowned and lauded novelist.

Unlike Mom, he came from extreme poverty, grew up on a farm in Ohio, spent all of his youth reading books and studying, to make sure that he never stepped foot or had to work hard in his life again.

There was an article in *Vanity Fair* a few years back, which said that he lived many lifetimes in one, and that his adventures, and his novels, and his life were something to be admired. I don't know whether the writer of that article was a friend of his, or just an admiring, aspiring novelist with stars in his eyes.

But the article even made his years of drug and alcohol addiction sound like something glamorous and fun to experience. I was pissed and fuming with anger when I read that and saw the cover at all the newspaper stands at the airports.

The managing editor wanted nothing to do with it because he had a big falling out with Dad. Apparently, Archibald Tanner threw a fit after the editor cut out some parts of the article that he'd submitted, called him names, and got himself fired.

When the editor came into the office the

following morning, he found little disposable cups filled with urine right outside his door.

As it turned out, Mom had more sway with the owners of the magazine than the editor because, I later found out, that she was the one who got that story about Archibald published in order to improve his image.

Of course, there was no proof that my father had anything to do with the cups, but he was seen in the building, and he had just gone on a loud, obnoxious, entitled rant, trying to get that editor fired.

These are the kinds of stories that never make it into the light of day because they're not glamorous and they're not fun. And no one wants to discuss the depths to which addiction will often lead you, and how little you will care, when you're down there, about your reputation or anything as consequential.

None of this is, of course, an excuse, and I'm not excusing him at all. I'm just trying to offer different facets of his personality, and explain why Lincoln got so mad at me when I compared him at all to our father.

I knock on the stall door and tell him to open it.

"Go away."

"Look, I wasn't comparing you to him as a man, not at all. I shouldn't have said that," I say, knowingly. "Okay. But you and I both know that he was a shitty father who worked all the time and eventually partied all the time."

"I don't party," Lincoln says.

He slams the stall door open so quickly that I practically jump out of the way.

"Do you know how many times the firm actually hired hookers to come to our floor and keep all of us *entertained*, so to speak? Just so that we're happy putting in a hundred hour weeks," Lincoln demands to know. "Do you know what that's like to be the only guy there who says no?"

"I'm sorry," I whisper.

"It's not about that. I'm not like that. I have my wife at home and I don't want to cheat on her. Do you know that they don't invite me out anymore? Do you know how much harder it is for me to make my career? You don't *fucking* know anything."

He points his finger in my face. I can't remember the last time I've seen him this angry.

"So, don't tell me that I'll be anything like our father. He's the scum of the earth. He never gave a shit about either of us. We could have been the kids of his housekeeper for all he cared. In fact, he probably treated them a little nicer."

"Look, I'm sorry," I say, shaking my head, suddenly filled with regret and contempt for what I said. "I know you're a good man, and I know that you're a good husband. And I know that you love Marguerite. But I also know that, just like me, you have something to prove. Marguerite made you ineligible for the money in that trust.

"There's six million dollars and I know that the reason why you're working so hard right now is try to make as much money as possible to prove our mom, our grandfather, everyone wrong. You're trying to make that money for yourself, but you don't need to. You have a beautiful wife. She loves you. She has loved you for years. You're going to have this child. You don't want to miss out on time with them just because you're trying to prove something to a ghost."

THE REST of dinner is pretty uneventful. We chitchat about nothing in particular and don't talk about our father again.

I get into a cab after saying goodbye and

promise to meet up with him this weekend for their baby announcement get-together. It's just going to be them, me, and our mom. I'm there as a buffer to keep her being cordial and nice.

I promise that I'll be there, and I hope that my presence will be enough, but I'm not sure.

When I sit down in the back of the cab, suddenly the quietness washes over me.

I give the driver the address and he drops me off in front of my building. I haven't been to this apartment in some time.

The last time I was in New York my client was near the private airport in the Hamptons, so I stayed in a hotel there. Walking back into this place I feel a little bit lost, and incredibly lonely.

On the outside, I like to pretend that I'm a man made of stone, steel, something indestructible.

But it's only because I'm trying to keep all the dysfunction of my family so tightly within myself and I'm about to explode.

There's glass everywhere. Mom had insisted that I get this condo because the building was just being built and it was going to be an architectural marvel, now it just feels like an aquarium if there were another building anywhere in sight.

There's only one real wall in the whole

apartment and that's when you walk in, everything else is glass.

It's a corner unit and I had to have specially installed blackout curtains just so I could sleep in the mornings. I'm above the cloud cover, deep within it, and it's generally the case almost every time I'm here. This building is too tall.

I don't like this place. I don't like the fact that it doesn't have room service and I don't like the empty refrigerator that has to stay empty because I'm never here long enough to fill it up.

It's not that I particularly love being catered to, it's more that it makes me feel like I have a place I belong. I can go down to the lobby, I can chitchat with the front staff. I can meet someone at a bar.

There's a gym and a pool and a restaurant downstairs. The restaurant is undergoing some renovations and hasn't been open for a while.

I plop down on the bed, dress clothes and all, and consider my options for the evening.

I could go out on the town, a club maybe, call a few friends, none who are probably available on such short notice, but at least I can give it a try.

Or I could go to Redemption.

Hmm, now there's an idea.

I feel my eyebrow rising, even considering the

concept. The last time I was there, wasn't particularly great, but I'm tempted to give it another shot.

Jacqueline has been haunting me a little bit less and less as I've been trying to put her out of my mind.

What if I were to just go, get really drunk, and not really pay attention to who I meet in the dark?

22

JACQUELINE

I see him from across the room. He walks in, broad shoulders, casual gray suit, no tie, starched white shirt, unbuttoned at the top, tan olive skin, looks good in the faint light.

He grabs a drink at the bar and then assesses the room. I'm sitting all the way in the corner, shrouded in darkness. He won't be able to see me unless he walks all the way over here.

My heart skips a beat when I see him.

He's here, he's here, I say excitedly to myself, but he doesn't know that I am here, and suddenly everything sinks to the pit of my stomach.

Dante's here to pick up someone else.

He's not here for me, of course not.

Why would he be? I feel like a fool, and that's just fine.

I'm used to feeling this way around guys, but something about him ... Suddenly, I feel nauseated.

I watch him walk around the room.

First, he swivels on the chair to survey the perimeter. He looks at faces. He watches bodies. He assesses his options, and then he moves casually to the lounge, walking slowly enough to start up a conversation with someone, but not pausing for anyone in particular.

And then, almost as if he knows that I'm here, he narrows his gaze on my section of the room, the corner that I was so certain that he wouldn't be able to see me in.

"Jacqueline," he says, walking up to me.

I sit up in my seat and he sits down. I don't invite him.

"It's nice to see you again."

I give him a slight nod, but say nothing.

He takes a sip of his whiskey, swirls the amber colored liquid at the bottom of his glass, and then looks up at me again.

"I was hoping I'd see you here."

With my gold mask on my lap, I feel exposed, but in a good way.

"I thought that we weren't supposed to know who we are," I say, pointing to the mask in his hand.

He shrugs. "I don't see you hiding."

"Well, I am in the corner, some would argue the opposite."

"I can leave if you want," he says, his eyes laser-focused on mine.

He waits for me to answer, and finally I manage to mumble, "No, it's fine."

I have looked for him here and I've thought about him so much, but then to suddenly see him before me, present and interested, caught me off guard.

Music starts to thump louder on the dance floor and I glance over at the bodies pressing and grinding against each other. Somewhere in that mosh pit is Allison, looking for her couple.

She promised me that she would be my wing woman and she'd abandoned me as quickly as she could.

We watch everyone dance, and at the end of the song, Cassandra comes to the microphone. Her voice is as smooth as ever and she announces that the Masquerade Ball festivities will be starting soon. I have no idea what this means and I'm a little scared to find out, and that fear, it's not entirely excitement. It's real fear.

Dante continues to sit next to me, observing the room, but saying nothing and not even trying to make conversation, and suddenly I feel very comfortable in the silence. It's relaxing and it makes my anxiety diminish just a little bit.

The tone of the light changes and people part down the middle. Cassandra, in her long flowing white gown hugging tightly around her hips and giving her the curvy figure of a 1950s movie star, stands in the front and says, "We're going to play a little game."

The excited crowd lets out thunderous, ferocious yelps, and Cassandra licks her bright red lips in anticipation.

"You have all been assigned numbers and when we call your number, please come to the stage."

I force myself further into the corner. I hold my number so tightly, the little piece of paper that it's on shrivels up into a scrap.

Suddenly, I get the feeling that the person who is least excited to be up there on stage is probably the one that's going to be chosen.

"2, 17, 33, 46," Cassandra reads out, holding a card in her hand.

The crowd breaks into applause and separates to let the people walk to the stage.

I see Allison in the crowd, right in front, and our eyes meet.

She waves me over.

I shake my head no.

"That's my friend," I tell Dante. "She's very excited to be here."

"Yeah, I can see that," he says, without making a move.

"Aren't you going to go up there for a better look?"

"Nope." He shakes his head. "This is the only view I need."

He stares at me in a disarming kind of way. The stare becomes impossible to bear and I look away, but I still feel it on me.

It throws my body into a flash of heat.

When Cassandra lifts her finger and her diamond necklace moves slightly, framing perfect breasts just so, the room quiets down and the people on the stage turn to look at the audience.

The guys seem more nervous than the girls, who look like they can't wait to get started.

Cassandra walks over with a box of cards. "Pull one out," she instructs, "and read what it says."

A big, voluptuous woman, tall with broad shoulders and an enormous blonde hairstyle, eagerly puts her hand inside. She pulls out a card and reads and screeches in excitement.

"What does it say?" Cassandra asks.

Silence falls.

"Take off a piece of clothing," the woman reads, her lips quivering.

"Can I take it off anyone up here?" she asks Cassandra.

"Yes, if they're willing."

Everyone nods in approval.

The woman walks back and forth, trying to decide, eventually settling on a slim redhead with A cups and bright, wide eyes. She walks around and unzips her floor-length gown and lets it fall to the floor. All that's left are panties and a bra.

The room cheers and the redhead blushes from a little bit of embarrassment, but then she spreads her legs out wide, puts her hands on her hips and walks around, showing them her curves. She even turns away from the crowd, bends over to show off her butt cheeks in the thong.

I glance at Dante.

It would be a lie to say that I wasn't aroused by this, just like everyone else in the room, but still my thoughts come back to him, who's just sitting here without saying a word.

I want him to invite me into the back, or better yet out, I want him to ask for my real name and my real phone number.

Suddenly I feel like such a fool, an idiot for thinking that he wants anything more than what we had before.

I have to put him out of my mind. I have to get away from this place. It's no longer for me. Without saying a word, I get up and start to walk away.

"Hey, where are you going?"

It takes Dante two big steps to catch up to me in my high heels.

"I have to go," I mumble.

There's no one at the coat check, so I just reach over and grab my jacket and walk out the front door.

A gust of wind blasts my face and I struggle to zip my jacket.

"Wait!" he yells after me as I rush down the street.

23

DANTE

I watch them dance and play a game onstage. Everyone watches. Everyone huddles around and waits for the next dress, next shirt to come off.

But they don't hold my attention. My gaze returns to Jacqueline.

I can feel her. I want her to feel me watching her, me wanting her.

We sit in silence, and in those few moments, I forget about everything else in my life.

It's just her.

I want to hold her. I want to touch her. I want to be with her.

The faint scent of her perfume excites me, and just as I'm about to say something, she storms off.

I follow quickly behind.

She grabs her jacket and runs out the door.

"Wait up!" I yell after her. "Wait."

But she doesn't, and she runs fast. Something drops out of my pocket and I turn back when I realize that it's my wallet. By the time I turn back and pick it up, she's gone.

No, no, no, I say to myself.

I walk briskly past one street then another, praying that she didn't hop into a car, and then just before I decide to turn around to check the other side, I see her on the other side of a narrow alley turning the corner.

Picking up my feet, I run fast, catching up.

"Jacqueline!"

When she turns around, her face is flushed. There's a little light illuminating us and the dark brick behind her looks wet.

"What do you want?" she demands to know, crossing her arms in front. She takes a step away from me, and when I take one forward, she takes another one back, her shoulders colliding with the wall.

"Why did you leave?"

"Because I wanted to."

She slides along the wall and starts to walk away. I'm tempted to reach out and grab her hand, but I don't want to scare her.

"Weren't you having fun?"

"Does it look like I'm having fun?" she snaps, her finger in my face, crinkling her nose. Two little lines form right in the middle of her forehead.

"What do you want?" she challenges me.

"I wanted to see you. That's why I came."

"Please." She tilts her head, rolling her eyes.

"Are you mad *at me*?" I ask.

I take a step away. My dress shoes make little clinking noises as I shuffle them against the asphalt. Suddenly, it begins to rain and little drops start falling from the sky.

"No, I'm not mad at you. I'm mad at myself."

"For what?"

She rubs her shoulders with her small, elegant hands, trying to warm up. Dressed in a short cocktail dress and slim heels, she shifts her weight from one foot to another to stay warm.

Her light brown hair was curlier and with a lot more body before, but after a jog and a little bit of moisture falling from the sky, the strands now fall flat around her face.

"What are *we* doing here?" Jacqueline asks. "*Why* did you follow me?"

Her nails are short, not acrylic, painted some sort of sparkly blue color. Though not exactly elegant, they show character and personality and I like that.

"I came here hoping I'd find you," I say.

Looking deep into her hazel eyes, I try desperately to convince her that I'm telling the truth.

"Yeah, right." She rolls her eyes. "You came to *Redemption*, a sex club, to look for me? I don't think so."

She turns to walk away, and this time I do grab her arm.

"I'm telling you the fucking truth," I hiss.

Her face falls just a little, and a small smile forms at the corner of her lips.

"After we met, I came back again," I explain in a more reserved tone of voice. "I met two beautiful women who wanted to spend the night with me, and I couldn't do it. I kept thinking about you and how they *weren't* you."

"You don't even know me," she says, raising one eyebrow and tucking a strand of hair behind her ear.

"I know. And I'd like to."

Jacqueline narrows her eyes, not exactly believing me, but not exactly *not* believing me either. "So what do you want to do now?" she asks.

"I want to ask you on a date."

24

JACQUELINE

Dante is driving me home. He had followed me out of the club and he told me that he came back looking for me. I was so angry at him. I was so angry at myself for being an idiot for wanting him and for coming here and looking for him, and I had no idea that he felt the same way.

And now, I'm sitting in his Maserati, and he's driving me to my mother's house in Jersey City. I told him that I can take a cab or a ride share, but he insisted, and I wanted to spend more time with him anyway.

His slightly curly, dark hair frames his face as he drives a little bit too fast down the empty streets.

I've never been in a car this expensive before, and if you thought that a Maserati or some other luxury vehicle looks good on the outside, it's hard to believe the features and the comfort that you experience inside.

The world ceases to exist, but not in any metaphorical sense. There's hardly any road noise at all, and you're just traveling in your own little sanctuary in total silence, unless of course you want to put on some music.

"How are you doing?" he asks, turning slightly to look at me.

"Good."

He smiles. His lips are luscious. His teeth are white and sparkle under the streetlights. He has a strong Roman nose and bright blue eyes that can be quite disarming and cold, but I don't feel anything but warmth right now.

I had already said yes to the date, but we haven't decided when or where.

"Tell me something true," Dante says.

"My real name is Jacqueline."

"My real name is Dante," he says, smiling.

I laugh and he laughs along with me. I put my hand on the hand rest and play with the buttons

without actually pressing one all the way down.
"What do you do for a living?" I ask again.

"Travel a lot. I work for a company that assesses
risk and invests in high-risk endeavors."

"Isn't that dangerous?" I ask.

"Yeah. You can lose a lot of money, but you can
also win big."

"So you didn't lie about that either?"

He shakes his head no.

"You know, we were supposed to tell each other
stories? You know, pretend to be these other
people."

"Yeah. I've been doing that a lot, and it was fun
and it has its place, but I didn't want to do that with
you."

"Why not?" I ask, picking up a strand of hair
that has hopelessly fallen and playing with it.

"I don't know. I just saw you out there and I
wanted to talk to you. And when I did, I didn't want
to lie, and that was that."

The GPS leads him straight to my house, and I
point it out. "It's the one with the big bushes out front."

"Looks like a nice place to live," he says, and I
turn to face him.

"I live with my mom."

"You do?"

"Yeah. She has cancer. She's getting treatment."

"Oh, I'm so sorry."

"Anyway, we'll be leaving on Monday to go to Minnesota. The Danick Clinic. She's getting an experimental surgery done."

"Oh, okay."

"So in terms of that, I'd like to go out with you, but I'm going to be in Minnesota for a while helping her with the recovery and everything else."

"Yeah, I get it. Let's exchange numbers and maybe make some plans."

"I don't think you understand. I think it's going to be like weeks, and tomorrow I have to spend all day packing, getting ready. The flight is really early in the morning."

"Are you trying to back out? If you're trying to back out, just tell me," he asks, suddenly insulted.

"No, not at all."

He turns the engine off and turns around in the seat to face me. "Please don't feel any pressure to go on a date with me. Okay?"

"I'm not making this up."

"I'm not saying that you are, but I just want to be honest."

"I want to see you. I'm just laying out my life for

the next month and the fact that I won't be here. That's it."

"And if I happen to be in the Midwest during that time?" he asks coyly.

"I'd love to see you." I nod.

Our eyes meet again and something in his changes. He looks down at my lips and then up at me asking permission.

I move a little bit closer and he does as well, and our lips touch again.

He reaches over and brushes his fingers along my neck, touching me slightly and sending shivers down my spine.

He kisses me over and over again, and I kiss him back. Our tongues find each other's, but it takes some time for me to pull away.

"I have to go," I say, shaking my head in the direction of my house.

"It was great to see you tonight," Dante says.

"You, too. Oh, wait, phone number," I say, slamming the door behind me but pointing my finger up in the air and leaning back over.

He opens the window and we exchange numbers.

When I wave goodbye to him, he tugs on my

arm, pulling me back inside and giving me another kiss.

"I'll be in touch," he promises.

My stomach is full of butterflies the whole time I walk up to the front door.

25

JACQUELINE

O ur arrival in Minnesota is pretty uneventful. After a lot of packing and sorting, trying to figure out just the right amount of stuff to bring, I finally settled on a large carry-on bag.

It's going to be a hospital, and I'm just going to be doing a lot of waiting and sitting around, and comfort at a difficult time is my number one priority. I pack a lot of leggings, loose fitting tops, sweaters, and comfortable shoes.

My mom on the other hand, seems to think that she's going to some sort of celebrity birthday bash, and packs herself heels, a big bag of makeup, all of her hair tools, and everything else that's completely unnecessary.

"Listen. A woman has to look good to feel good," she said. "After I get all of this packing done, I think we should celebrate."

I love her attitude, but I don't quite agree with it. It's not that I don't pay attention to my looks. It's just that ... Well, yeah, I don't really pay that much attention to my looks.

We fly coach, sit next to each other, and Mom manages to fall asleep while I listen to music and think about Dante.

What were the chances of him being at Redemption?

What are the chances of him actually telling me the truth?

On one hand, I hate this excited thirteen-year-old girl that I've suddenly become.

But on the other hand, this is the happiest that I've felt since Michael's death, and I can't help but want to revel in it.

I thought for sure that after he dropped me off, he'd play some game, the way that guys play where he will wait a requisite amount of time to call me to not look "desperate".

But he didn't.

He texted me that night, and again the following day. We texted quite a lot on Sunday, and

I promised to be in touch after we land and get situated in Minnesota.

We arrive in Minneapolis around ten in the morning, grab some breakfast at the airport Starbucks, and take the rental car to the apartment complex that's walking distance to the hospital.

The hospital is not located in the city, but rather near a cute little town with shops and a main street called Aspinwall. I like that. As I wheel my mom's heavy suitcase to our first floor apartment, I see two little girls playing on the playground in the park across the way.

The pre-teens laugh and joke without a care in the world, and I suddenly feel incredibly jealous. If this were a big city hospital, there would be a big trauma unit, a big ER to accommodate gunshot wound victims, and all of the medicine that big city hospitals usually deal with. But here in the middle of this bucolic little town I feel like my pain and my mom's suffering doesn't belong.

Everyone is happily going along with their day, living their lives, and we are these imposters, occupying an apartment on the corner, and filling it with grief.

My mom and I go to her first preliminary appointment which is just a meeting with the doctor at her office. It's a corner glass unit with a view of the rose garden below.

Dr. Ellis is a no-nonsense kind of personality who immediately puts me at ease. She doesn't sugarcoat things, but she isn't overly morose either.

She lays out the possibilities, and the options, and all of the details about the surgery, 99% of which goes over my head.

"So what are the chances of this being successful?" I ask.

"It's about fifty-fifty. We don't have a good number of cases and subjects who have gone through it. And as you know, medicine is an art as well as a science. People come with their own histories and different speeds at which their cells mutate. You're doing a good job of following the right diet, but it all has to do with how your body reacts and that we don't know for sure."

"So what is the process for the surgery?" I ask, my hands trembling. I stick them deep into my pockets to keep them out of view.

"Well, after this you'll go and get all your blood drawn, and tomorrow morning you need to be there at eight o'clock for prep. Surgery's probably going to start around 10:30, 11:00, and we'll go from there."

We both nod, both probably feeling tense and anxious, but relieved at the same time.

In situations like these it's important to have something to do.

You got this diagnosis but what do you do now?

How do you try to *deal* with it?

This procedure has given my mom and me a lot of hope, and it's not for naught. I'm thankful that even if things don't work out well, I have this good feeling of hope to hold on to at this moment.

While my mom is getting her blood drawn and I sit in the waiting room, Dante calls me.

"How's it going?" I fill him in on everything that has happened and then realize that maybe this is just too much information.

"Maybe I shouldn't be telling you all this."

"Why not?" he asks.

"I don't know…but we haven't even been on our first date yet, and it feels like I'm talking to you like we've been dating for three months."

"What if we just fast-forward?" Dante asks.

That catches me by surprise. I shuffle my feet along the linoleum floor and run my finger over the same piece of dry paint on the wall.

"Look, I like you a lot," Dante continues. "This is happening in your life, and I want to know what's going on. It's up to you to tell me or not, but I'm here to listen."

The words hit just the right spot. I suddenly get completely overwhelmed and tears start to stream down my cheeks.

"Are you okay? What's going on?"

"No, I'm just ... I'm just …" I choke up. "That was just such a nice thing to say. I had ... I don't know. That was just a really good thing to say."

I find myself repeating my words over and over. When Mom comes out from the back office I tell him that I have to go.

"How did everything go?" I ask.

"Fine. All done for today. Now, I just have to wait for tomorrow. What should we do tonight?"

"Anything you want," I say.

"Okay." Mom smiles mischievously. "Then tell me about this guy you've been talking to."

26

JACQUELINE

Mom wants to know about Dante. It's hard for me to figure out what I should and shouldn't say. I gloss over some details.

At first, I pretend like what we have is no big deal, but she doesn't buy it. She knows that I'm acting differently. She knows that I'm waiting around for a call and I'm texting a lot.

We order pizza and sit in the makeshift temporary living room. It feels a lot like a long-term stay hotel. I tell Mom that I met Dante at a club, not mentioning any specifics.

She knows that I've been going out a lot ever since we lost Michael, meeting lots of strangers, assuming that he's just one of many. But she suspects that something is different about him.

"Tell me what he's like," she asks.

"Mysterious," is the only thing I can say.

It feels so cliche and yet that's really the only word for it. I tell her what he does for a living.

"Well, I'm glad that you have something interesting happening," Mom says. "It's important. You haven't dated anyone in a while."

"Yeah. I know." I wave my hand.

"Listen, I worry about that kind of thing. You know, you're my child and I want you to be happy."

"Please, the next thing that you're going to say is that I'm getting up there in age."

"No, not at all, but having a long-term committed relationship can be very fulfilling. You'll have someone to support and love you. I want that for you."

Before Dad became a gambler and an addict, he was a journalist. I followed in his footsteps and sometimes I hate that. My resentments toward him are innumerable, but he's still my father and I still miss him.

My mom met my dad on campus at the University of Florida. She went there to get away from the cold winters. My father drove down from

Michigan to meet some girls and occasionally go to class. He was always really into the partying and not so much into the studying.

He got a scholarship and he met the most unlikely woman to steal his heart, my mom, who would usually spend the weekends at the library. The fact that she turned him away multiple times made him flock to her like a moth to a flame. He liked the challenge. He liked that she said no. He told me this many times.

Eventually he brought her out of her shell. She was shy and awkward, a little scrawny with thick bottle cap glasses and frizzy hair that the humidity did no favors for.

He invited her to his parties. He introduced her to his friends and she changed, but in a good way. She didn't change who she was, but she found that she could be someone who was fun and outgoing and the life of the party if she wanted to. That's what she always told me she loved most about Dad at that time. He made it okay for her to take chances. He made it a safe place for her to fall.

He worked as a promoter at clubs, trying to bring in the local crowds. They started out as friends, but after a while, they became closer than that. He took her to see Bob Dylan.

They first hooked up during spring break when Dad was booking a bunch of local clubs. He was working around the clock as the kids partied and Mom helped him put out the pamphlets. There was a time before the internet where you had to hand deliver fliers and actually entice people to come in by standing out front.

As it turned out, Mom was able to become somewhat of an extrovert at this time. She told me about how she got her hair done and would have a few shots to "take off the edge." And after that, she would loosen up.

"She just needed a little liquid courage," Dad said.

For someone like my mom, who's naturally shy, alcohol allowed her to open up and realize that people weren't at all that scary.

Back then Dad's drinking was just social. He knew how to have a good time, but he never blacked out like a lot of his other friends did. He'd have a few beers and he'd nurse one the rest of the night just to keep the party going.

Mom always talked about those days very fondly.

I guess, many people feel that way about

college, but for her, college was where she met the love of her life.

We talk about Dad again. Not the dad from the later years, but the dad that I knew a little bit as a kid and the dad that Michael loved.

This was the dad who taught us how to ride a bike and the importance of always wearing a helmet.

This was the dad who took us hiking and taught us how to ski.

This was the dad that I want back in my life. This was the dad and the husband that I wish my mom had now.

Even now, despite everything that happened, I know that what they had was real.

I know that what they had was real love. It just got all fucked up, the way that love sometimes gets when it's thrown into the real world with all of its problems and addictions and lies.

27

DANTE

I arrive on Cape Cod on a particularly gloomy, overcast day. The weather continues to threaten to break into rolling thunderstorms, but nothing happens except for low-hanging clouds and a bunch of drizzle.

Some of my fondest memories of growing up are at this estate. There's a main four-bedroom home that Mom occupies as well as two guest cottages for overnight guests whenever she has family or friends over.

Every time I come back here, I feel like it becomes a time warp. This is the house where I spent the first seven years of my life.

This is home.

We traveled to and from and had an apartment

in New York and a house in the South of France, but this is what I always thought of when I thought of *home*.

My mom grew up here. While her parents were away having fun in the big city, this is the place where she lived with her nanny, the woman she always thought of as her real mother.

Mom employed some help, a housekeeper and a few others, a gardener, of course, someone to take care of the pool and the grounds, and we had babysitters when she needed to leave us, but we never had an official nanny. She was the one that was there until she wasn't.

I was seven when she announced that she was sending me away to boarding school.

As I walk through the rose garden leading up to the green door with the giant antique gold knocker, I have a flashback of standing right here and crying, begging her to let me stay.

I thought she was sending me away because I was bad. I thought that she no longer wanted to be my mom.

I was scared, terrified of going to this place with strangers taking care of me.

The first year was pretty rough, I'm not going to lie. But I got used to it and after a while I even enjoyed it and I didn't want to come home, and that made Mom mad.

"Hey, you're here!" Mom runs in, draping her arms around my neck, dressed in a Chanel suit with her hair recently styled.

She looks at least twenty years younger than she actually is.

"Your brother isn't here yet, so we'll have some time to gossip and catch up."

She leads me to the recently remodeled farmhouse-style kitchen with blue cabinets on the bottom and white ones on top, with thick, antique style pulls in matte black.

"This place looks nice," I say, walking around and feeling the quartz underneath my fingertips.

"Well, you know. I get sick of having the exact same thing all the time."

"Are you redoing everything?" I ask.

"No, not at all. Just the kitchen and one of the guest houses. I don't think I want to do anything with the upstairs quite yet."

The house itself is a quintessential Cape Cod home. It has a broad frame with a moderately steep-pitched gable roof, a large central chimney, and very low on ornate extravagances.

I walk over to the sliding glass door in the living

room and look out at the meadow out front. The Olympic-sized swimming pool is over to one side, covered up and winterized until Memorial Day. The meadow and the trees are out in the distance along with the cliffs and the roaring ocean reminding me of the life that I used to have here and all the games that my brother and I played.

"So, what's going on? What's new?" Mom asks, rubbing my hand.

"Nothing." I shrug. "I mean, we just talked. How about you?"

"I'm working on a bag line: totes, purses."

"Really?" I act like I'm surprised, but I'm not.

My mom has always had a number of entrepreneurial projects in the works at the same time. A lot of them have been quite successful.

Back in the nineties, she started a jeans line. Her fellow socialites were appalled and there was a lot of gossip, but when she made close to a hundred million dollars and promoted it on *The Today Show* and *Good Morning America*, they all jumped in on the idea and started their own clothing brands.

"So bags? Purses?" I ask.

"Yeah. Well, you know how much I love purses, and I still have all my contacts with the jean manufacturers since I still have a twenty percent stake in the business. I figured why not try to do something in textiles? Just a little bit different, since I can't compete with my own property, as you know."

I nod approvingly.

On the outside, my mom seems flighty and the type of person that goes wherever the wind takes her, but in reality, she's very focused, very serious, and if she has gone so far as to tell me about it, it's probably been in the works for months.

"Well, let me know, because anything I can do to help. I'd love to see some of your designs."

"I thought you'd never ask." Her eyes light up.

Following her upstairs, I step on the riser, and I remember that this is the exact spot where Lincoln pushed me when we were kids.

We fought a lot, arguing about anything and everything but mostly competing for attention from our mom.

Of course, I didn't know that at the time. All I knew was that he was in my life too much and she wasn't there at all.

I don't know exactly what precipitated that particular push, but I remember finding myself at the bottom of the stairs, a big gash in my forehead and right above my eye, followed by a trip to the emergency room for seven stitches.

Lincoln was grounded for a couple of weeks, but that hardly bothered him since he stayed in his room, watched television, and played hours and hours of video games anyway.

My mom's office is upstairs overlooking a beautiful sycamore tree with a bench curving around the trunk. Our old Golden retriever, Molly, is buried under that bench and we put it up in her memory. I still can't look at it without my heart closing up tightly.

The office has built-in bookshelves on both sides, filled with mementos and books, as well as boxes of craft projects and art supplies. Ten years ago, Mom started painting and has actually moved her studio to the other guest bedroom down the hall because the paintings were big and took up so much space.

I've always admired her ability to stay busy in one place. She will just toil around this house doing kitchen remodels, working on her paintings, designing clothes, gardening, swimming, throwing a few parties, but all in all, she's a huge homebody, at least at this point in her life.

I, on the other hand, have to be constantly on

the move. I get on flights, I live in hotel rooms, I work too many hours all in an effort to stay busy, or maybe just occupied.

I exist on a treadmill, not going anywhere in particular but I press on because it's really just the physical act of changing locations that's important.

Mom has a large collection of sample bags ranging from simple tote bags with minimalist, elegant designs to high-end purses for a more elegant and dressed up feel.

"The only thing I would say besides the fact that they're all really well-made and have excellent craftsmanship is that they don't fit with each other."

"What do you mean?" She tilts her head to one side.

"They just sort of feel like they belong to two different brands."

"Yeah, I had the same feeling. One feels like it's Saks Fifth Avenue, and the other is a little bit more casual, a cross between Free People and Target."

"Exactly." I nod. "I mean, both are great but you should figure out where you stand. Do you have a concept for the company as a whole?"

"No, that's what I'm working on. I wanted to make all the samples first, see how I felt about them and then decide which route to go."

"I'd really just pick one at first and stick to it. Build a good audience, a good mailing list, successful Facebook advertising campaign, Instagram, that whole thing prior to expanding. And if you want to go high-end, I mean, you definitely can charge more, but it's a different market, as you know. And then of course there's the sort of Nordstrom prices, high-end but not ridiculous."

She nods. "Yeah. Pricing and positioning the company will be the key thing here."

"Couldn't agree more," I say. "Once you have more ideas or maybe a layout for your website, I could take a look. I know that you don't necessarily need investment, but I've had my investors put money into Meg and we've been quite successful."

"*Meg*? You invested in *Meg*?" She gasps.

"Yeah. You know it?" I ask, genuinely surprised.

"Of course I know it! I'm in the fashion industry. They're top of the line. They have none of that fast fashion crap that just pollutes all of the landfills in the world. They're actually able to give people a good price and make a hefty profit."

"That's what I thought, too." I smile. "That's why we invested. I mean, who doesn't want Target or TJ Maxx prices with designer quality?"

28

DANTE

After my conversation with Mom, she's on cloud nine: excited, jubilant, confident in her designs. Obviously, decisions have to be made about the direction of this fledgling company, but she appreciates my approval, not just because I'm her son, but because I'm a man.

Despite all of her experiences and confidence as a woman, I know that she's seeking out, and perhaps will always be seeking out the approval of men that have no business approving anything that she does or doesn't do with her life.

Lincoln and Marguerite have arrived while we were upstairs, and Mom made no rush to greet them.

"Lina will show them in," Mom says when I mention this fact.

At first I'm concerned but, after talking to her about her purses, I'm glad that I could lift her spirits up a little bit prior to seeing Lincoln and Marguerite.

When we get downstairs, Lincoln is getting a beer out of the fridge. Mom immediately makes a face when she sees Marguerite. It's rather subtle, but I notice it. The thing about her is that once she writes you off as someone who is a less than an acceptable choice for one of her sons, there's little that anyone can do.

Marguerite had the unfortunate experience of meeting Mom in college, dressed in sweats. Mom had dropped by and Marguerite just happened to be there studying in his room, hair unwashed, face without makeup. It was just a typical Tuesday night study session at Yale. And yet, for some reason, Mom couldn't grasp that concept.

I give them both hugs. Marguerite holds a glass of water, takes a sip, and cuts herself a lemon wedge.

"How are you feeling?" I ask and her eyes immediately flash up to me.

"Fine. Fine. Everything's great," she says a little too quickly.

I was asking about the pregnancy, of course, but trying not to be too obvious.

"How's work?" I ask.

"Busy, tiring, but very rewarding," Marguerite says.

"So what kind of things do you usually do at the ER?" Mom asks after a cool hello.

She pours herself a glass of lemonade and offers us some as well, but we all decline.

She ushers us to the sitting room that's rarely used except for occasions like these and sits down in her grand white linen chair with a big oil painting of herself in a ravishing red gown. There's a little black dog by her feet who belonged to a neighbor, but whom Mom loved.

She loved him so much that she included him in the painting instead of us, who were just kids then.

You can read into that as much as you like, but I choose not to.

Marguerite sits right next to Lincoln, placing her hands on the edge of her knees. She actually watched a number of YouTube videos about how to be a lady in order to make a better impression on our mom.

She learned not to cross her legs at the knees, but rather at the ankles, sit up straight, wear nude nail polish. In my opinion, she basically learned how to get rid of every part of her personality just to appease some person that honestly could never be appeased.

Lincoln exchanges looks with his wife, and I take a sip of my beer knowing that it's about to begin.

After a little bit of chitchat, he launches into it.

"Mom, we wanted to tell you that we have some great news."

She sits up a little straighter and raises one eyebrow.

"Oh, yes?"

"Yes, Marguerite and I are expecting a baby," he says and her face falls. With her lips tensing up, forming a slim straight line across her face, she looks like she's about to say something incredibly mean.

Glancing over at me, I give her a smile of encouragement, but when I realize that she's a little bit slow on the reaction time, I stand up and embrace both of them with a big bear hug.

"Oh my God! I'm so happy for you guys. When

are you due?" I ask, pretending that I don't already know.

"October," they say, beaming.

I hug and congratulate them again and again, trying to fill the room with my own happiness to make up for my mom's lack thereof.

———

IT TAKES Mom a few moments to recover her composure. She quickly paints a smile on her face and gives both of them a hug.

I hope that they can't tell, but I sense some hesitation. Still, there's only so much they can do and so much that they can expect from her.

For now, it seems to be enough.

Right before dinner is served, my phone rings and I have to take it.

"We're going to be sitting down," Mom scolds me like a child.

"Listen, this is work. I'll make it quick. I promise."

"Hey, how's it going, Cedar?" I ask.

"How's it going?" he roars into the phone. "I talked to Vasko again and he said that you never called him back."

My jaw tightens up.

"Listen, I went over the financials, taking out what I thought about Vasko personally, and that company just doesn't make sense. There's so much money going out and then a bunch coming in from unusual sources."

"So what are you trying to say?" Cedar asks.

His voice sounds gruff on the phone and I can practically hear him sucking down a cigarette and smell the bourbon on his lips.

"I don't want the investors to put their money with Vasko. I'm not going to make that recommendation," I say, standing firm. "I wasn't lying when I said that I went over the financials again and there were a lot of red flags. It's almost as if the entire company is some sort of shell organization."

"Listen, you don't have a choice on this one," Cedar says, moving in his chair as I hear that loud creaking sound of oak and leather underneath his substantial mass. "This is going to happen. We're going to invest with Vasko."

I pause for a moment. I've walked into another room, the library with old leather bound editions, many of them quite rare and signed by authors.

Cedar has never talked to me this way. I was

always the one in charge of the investors that I brought in and the ones that were assigned to me. My entire job is to use what I know and my own intuition to decide whether or not to trust a certain company with our money.

This is very subjective work, but I've become quite good at it over the years. Often investing in businesses that are fledgling, but had the type of CEOs who would go to the ends of the earth to grow their sales and to become successful.

I saw none of that in Vasko. He is lazy and bored.

It's almost as if he was handed the company by someone else and told to run it and he has no idea what he's doing.

I go over all of this with Cedar.

He listens as I pace around the lacquered, hardwood floors, feeling the material of the twelve-foot French imported curtains sewn with silk thread.

This is part of the house that retained its original charm. There's a large oak desk in the corner, looking out onto the pond outside. This is the place where I would sit as a kid and read every Isaac Asimov book I could find, imagining worlds filled with spaceships, aliens, and large intergalactic battle scenes.

"Listen, I know that you and I have not had any problems up until this point, but I'm not budging on this. Dante, you either call Vasko back and tell him that we're going to be starting the onboarding sequence or I'm going to find someone else who can do it. And then I can't make you any promises about keeping your job."

I press my hand so hard on the table that my knuckles turn white.

This is an ultimatum. It's either invest five million of investors' money who trusted me with it or get fired.

"You have twenty-four hours to decide," Cedar says and hangs up.

I stare at the phone for a few moments, looking out onto the pond. Two ducks float around on the partially frozen lake, one following the other without a care in the world.

29

DANTE

The sun has been hidden behind clouds all day and when sunset comes, very little changes, except it gets slightly darker. Someone clears their throat behind me and when I turn around, I see that it's Lina, my mom's faithful housekeeper, who has been with her since I was a little kid. She's older now, but still wears her hair in a tight bun and has the same no-nonsense expression on her face.

She has worked here since moving from Brazil in her early thirties, leaving behind her baby with her parents and sending the majority of her paycheck back to give them a better life.

"Your mom is asking for you," Lina says in a very slight accent.

In addition to speaking Portuguese, she's also fluent in German, English, and Spanish, having studied linguistics at university.

Someone from the outside might wonder why she has been a housekeeper for so many years, but I think it's because Mom is very generous and loyal.

When it comes to people she likes, Mom likes to provide. She doesn't expect her to work long hours and she isn't particularly picky. Plus Lina gets to live in the one-bedroom cottage just across the meadow for free, and that kind of accommodations would go for about three grand a month in the winter, and who knows how much during the high season.

Over the years, Lina and Mom have become close friends. They even have an informal book club on Thursday nights, discussing the latest Oprah recommendations.

I give Lina a smile and a hug when I approach her and ask her about Tanya, her daughter, who's now living in New York City and trying to be an actress.

Lina rolls her eyes, slightly annoyed.

"I did not come to this country to have my daughter try to become a Broadway star. She's not even in Los Angeles, trying to get onto a soap opera, which would have steady work."

"Well, you remember you took her to all those plays and musicals when she was a kid?"

"Yes, to show her *culture*," she says, throwing her hands in the air, "not to encourage her to become an artist or, God forbid, an actress."

I laugh and she laughs as well. She's only half serious.

Secretly, I think that she's proud that her daughter would risk so much in pursuit of her dreams. It reminds me a lot of what her mother did coming all the way to New England from a small, poor village in Brazil, but it's not my place to point this out.

I return back to the dining room where Mom has had more than a few cocktails and is suddenly acting very friendly with Marguerite.

"You know you're going to have to get a bigger apartment. I mean, one bedroom with a baby? That's pretty much as close to hell as you can get."

Marguerite smiles and laughs. "Actually it's a two bedroom."

Mom narrows her eyes.

"No, it's not. The other is Lincoln's office."

"Well, yes, but technically we have a bedroom and another bedroom that we've converted to his office, but it's not going to be that way for long."

"And where's Lincoln going to work when he's home?" Mom asks.

"We are hoping that he can take some time off and you know, really be there for the baby the first year."

Mom glares at Lincoln who shrugs his shoulders and looks away.

"And you're okay with this?" she asks.

Lincoln looks torn and needs a way out.

"Listen, Mom, we can talk about all of this later, let's just celebrate," I say. "There's going to be a baby in the family, a little grandchild. I mean, how exciting is that? I can't wait to meet my niece or nephew. Do you know what it's going to be yet?"

They shake their heads.

"What does that mean?" I ask. "Do you know and not telling, or do you actually not know?"

"We don't know," Lincoln says. "We want it to be a surprise."

Mom rolls her eyes and drinks the last of her wine quickly filling it back up. "You know, in my day we couldn't wait to figure out what we would have in order to decorate the rooms properly and everything else that goes into setting up for the baby's arrival. And now you have all of these medical tests at your service and you could find out the sex at like what… ten weeks? Twelve weeks? Who knows? And you're not taking advantage. That's just… I don't know."

"Isn't it a little romantic?" Marguerite asks. "I mean, there are so few surprises left in the world."

Mom leans over the table, just a little bit, holding her fork and knife properly in each hand. She looks like she's about to say something nice. I hold my breath.

And she says, "In 1968, my husband went out to get a pack of cigarettes and some milk and he never came home. How about that for a surprise?"

Silence falls over the table.

Mom cuts a little piece of salmon, drizzles it with lemon and pops it into her mouth.

The three of us sit still, trying to figure out how to respond or whether a response is needed at all.

LATER THAT NIGHT, long after Mom goes to sleep, and after Lincoln and I have a few more cocktails and talk about old times, I head up to the guest room two doors down from the main bedroom and open my laptop.

I want to go through Vasko's financials again

more thoroughly. I've had a few drinks and the numbers all blend together. Despite that the returns are paltry, they seem to be going around through various rounds of investment, just trying to raise money.

But where's the money going? I can't find out exactly.

The expenses are very vague.

The companies that the money's paid to seem shady as well, more like shell companies than anything else.

To get to the bottom of this would require the work of a private financial investigator.

But I have until tomorrow to decide.

Cedar has never made that kind of threat to me before. I have worked at this company for years. I have brought in a number of investors and the companies that we invested in have sold for millions and millions, bringing us massive profits along with a number of happy angel investors and their friends.

If I were to invest in Vasko, I would put my reputation on the line. In this business, my reputation is all I have.

But Cedar is my boss, the owner, and if he says

that we need to invest and that he'll fire me if we don't, then I don't exactly have a choice.

I don't want to talk loudly on the phone and I have a hard time modulating the sound of my voice after a little bit of alcohol.

I take my phone out for some fresh air.

I haven't been to the coast in ages and the walk is only a quarter of a mile away. I make my way through the meadow, past the weeping willows, and finally onto the rugged coastline of Cape Cod, filled with swaying grasses and dunes of sand. The stars are out and the sky is clear for once. But an arctic blast chills me to my bones even though I'm wearing a hefty winter jacket.

I scramble over the dunes, trying to find the path which had been swept over with sand and snow. When I finally get to the shoreline and see a figure walking in the distance.

Who could that be?

This isn't a private beach, but about as close to being private as you can get. The nearest house is five acres away and no one is usually around this time of year, except for my mom and a few other locals.

I pick up my feet.

Gaining ground, she hears me and when she turns back to look at me, moonlight hits her face and I see that it's Marguerite.

30

DANTE

"Hey, what's up? Is everything okay?" I break into a jog to catch up even though she averts her face and speeds up.

"What's wrong?" I ask when I get to her.

Marguerite's nose is a little runny, but she doesn't look like she's been crying.

"Why are you all the way out here? It's so cold. I thought you went to bed."

"I can go on a walk if I want. I don't need your permission," she snaps.

"I'm sorry, I didn't mean anything by…" My voice trails off.

She is right, of course. It's none of my business.

I take a few steps back and let her get ahead, but she turns back on her heels.

"Listen, I'm sorry for snapping. I just needed to leave that house. Your mom is very difficult to deal with."

Marguerite and I were pretty close when they first started dating, but over the years, we sort of drifted apart. The only time we ever saw each other was when they were a couple doing couple things. If I were ever alone with one of them, it was always my brother. Talking to her like this feels a little odd.

"Thanks for coming out...to Cape Cod, I mean," she says, gesturing for me to keep walking. "This whole announcement would have been so much harder if you weren't here."

I nod.

"You like to go out on walks in freezing cold weather?" I ask.

"I need some fresh air and to get my steps in, especially when I'm having a hard day and I can't have alcohol." Marguerite checks her Apple Watch.

"I just realized this was probably the first time that you've interacted with her without being properly lubricated and that can be quite challenging." I laugh.

"You have no idea. Plus with the pregnancy hormones, I'm just really out of whack."

We walk for a little bit listening to the sound of our footsteps against the wet sand.

"What are you doing here?" she asks.

"I need to make this phone call that I'm really dreading. Had a little bit too much to drink, so just trying to, you know, freshen up."

"Yeah. That sucks." She nods.

"Listen, I'm really happy for you," I say, putting my hand on her forearm.

She's dressed in multiple layers and a thick puffy coat, but she still looks small and a lot like the girl I met in college: a little too studious, a little nerdy, perfect for my brother, but not exactly the pristine daughter-in-law that my mom was always hoping for.

"I wouldn't let you do this alone," I say. "I hope that you two remember that when it's my turn."

"Your turn for what?"

"Well, you know, if I ever meet anyone."

"Oh my God," Marguerite says sarcastically, throwing her mittened hand on her chest. "Dante Langston has met someone special?"

"No, I'm not saying that."

I add quickly.

"You have to tell me about her!"

"I don't know what you're talking about," I backtrack, but not too well.

"I've known you long enough. You're like this George Clooney bachelor-type. So to have you even mention that there might be someone that you might bring home and subject to your mother… That's, God, I feel bad for her," she adds.

We both crack up laughing.

"Okay, maybe I like her too much to do that to her," I say.

"No, seriously, tell me about her," Marguerite says after a moment.

"She's very nice, sweet. We met at a club. Had this thing where neither of us were really making any long-term plans."

"Oh, really? You, not wanting something serious? I'm shocked," she says, her voice dripping in sarcasm.

"I'll ignore that," I say with a coy smile, returning to the story. "I ran into her again and we started spending time together. I don't know, I just feel different about her. Like I'm waiting for her to call. I want to text her. I feel like an idiot most of the time."

"You know what this means, right?" Marguerite

says, just as a strong gust of wind collides with our faces. "You're in love!"

She pulls her scarf up a little bit and I can barely hear her over the howls. I bend my body into the wind to keep it from toppling me over.

Despite what Marguerite might think, I don't think I'd be able to have this conversation anywhere else. Somehow the wind and the noise and all of the physical obstacles make me feel comfortable about talking to her about something so private.

If we were back home with a cup of tea and her eyes were on mine the whole time, I wouldn't be able to be as honest.

"Her mom is really sick," I finally say, "Cancer. They're trying experimental treatments in Minnesota, but I've read about them and chances aren't great."

"Oh, wow."

"Her brother just died a few months ago. So she's going through a lot," I add.

"Wow. You know, I wouldn't recommend you start your first serious relationship with someone who's going through so much. Despite how you feel about her."

"Why is that?" I ask, nodding.

"Because you're kind of a fuck-up," Marguerite

says a little too quickly. "You have a lot of issues and if you're not ready for something serious with her, then don't keep her waiting. Be honest. Tell her straight up. Tell her you're not interested."

I push my hands deep into my pockets. She's right. I know that she's right.

"Are you having some doubts?" she asks.

I shrug.

"You are, aren't you?"

"No, I'm not having doubts about *Jacqueline*. I'm just…you know, you're right. I haven't really dated anyone that much."

It was always a rule of mine to not get involved, not be looking for someone, but maybe it was just that I never connected with anyone before.

We walk a little bit further and the sand gets deeper and more difficult to wade through. When we turn around, the wind immediately dies down and suddenly we don't have to shout to hear each other.

"You know, I wasn't sure if I wanted to have kids," Marguerite says, rubbing her hands together to stay warm. "I mean, I love Lincoln and you know that we've been together for ages, but I was always really hesitant about children. I wasn't sure that it was something I wanted to do. I wanted to be a doctor and I am one, but the hours are hard. Seeing all that trauma in the emergency room, it takes a toll on you."

"I can only imagine," I say.

"Lincoln works such crazy hours. I just don't know how we're going to make this work."

"You're just going to have to work less and prioritize your family for a little while. Or you can get help."

"Help is definitely an option. But I just want us both to be there, you know? Like experience raising our child ourselves. But maybe that's just me talking right now and in six months I'll be running for the hills."

"Yeah, probably," I say and we both laugh.

"But this could be a really good bonding experience, not just with a baby, but with us."

"Have you talked to him about taking some time off?" I ask.

"He wants *me* to take time off, but he doesn't want to take time off *himself*. He wants to work more hours. He says that I could hire someone. And of course we can hire a nanny, but it wouldn't be a big deal if he cut back to what, sixty hours, just for a little while."

"Lincoln is a workaholic," I say. "It's kind of like a family curse."

"Yeah, I know. You guys have all this money and you still just can't stop working. What's that about?"

Now it's my turn to laugh.

"Lincoln and I are very different," I say, slowing down and turning to face her.

"We're really different, but we're also alike. You know? Trying to prove something to people who are no longer here. When you come from a wealthy family, you either sit around, do nothing all the time or you spend all of your hours trying to chase ghosts and show them that you can do just as much as they did. I think that's where he's coming from."

"Maybe you're right," Marguerite says, biting her lower lip. "Or maybe it's just losing the trust fund money."

31

DANTE

There are lots of Fifth Avenue and Park Avenue women who spend all their time going to lunch and planning parties while their husbands golf and act like masters of the universe on Wall Street, but Marguerite is nothing like that.

She went to medical school, did internships and a residency, and works crazy hours despite Lincoln making half a million and who knows how much more with bonuses every year.

They have not been in need of money for a long time. I have known Marguerite long enough to know that she's the least money hungry person out there.

She doesn't care about brands.

She doesn't care about designer things.

She likes things to be nice, but Target-nice. Not Saks Fifth Avenue or Bergdorf Goodman nice.

The issue with the trust fund isn't just about the six-million dollars.

"I talked to Lincoln already, and I know that he's no longer technically eligible for the trust, but the thing about the trusts is that they have to be taken to court and evaluated," I offer. "All it says is that he has to marry someone from a comparable family. Who knows what *that* means?"

"It means that I have to be rich. It means that when we're married, our incomes have to come together and make more money," Marguerite says, tilting her head. "You know that."

"But it has never been challenged in court, okay? Somebody wrote that decades ago to try to protect us from marrying women who would only be after our money. That is clearly not the case for you."

She shrugs and tries to walk away, but I pull her back.

"Our grandfather was just trying to look out for his fortune. He had no idea that his grandson would marry someone like you with your own career and income."

"Are you trying to take a side in all of this?" Marguerite says, folding her arms across her chest.

"No, not at all. All I'm trying to say is that it is worth pursuing because nothing is set in stone."

"What about your mom? How would she feel about us suing her for all of that money?"

"Technically not her, but the estate," I point out. "Yeah, that's not going to help your relationship. I don't know how she's going to feel, but probably not good, but you know what? You have nothing to prove. And if you did, you already proved it many years ago. You and Lincoln are solid and now you're having a child."

She shakes her head, still frustrated and annoyed.

"You're an established physician. You make your own money. I don't know what there is to prove," I continue. "I don't know why the trustees wouldn't agree to giving you the trust fund."

Marguerite inhales and exhales very slowly. "I don't either, except Lincoln is pretty sure that we are never going to get it."

"And if you don't?" I ask.

She glares at me and it feels like bullets hitting my body.

"I didn't mean it like that. I just meant… what if you don't get the six-million dollars, what then? Lincoln makes good money. You do as well. You have a career. You have the house in the Hamptons."

"Which your mom pays for," she adds. "That's the thing. Your mom is always trying to pull all these strings. It's like, we're her puppets. He makes his own money, so do I, but we couldn't afford that house in the Hamptons for the summer weekends. But why shouldn't we use it?"

It's more of a rhetorical question but she answers it before I can.

"Should we not use it just out of pride when your mom bought it in *our* names? She's paying the mortgage. Still, every time I'm there, I feel like I owe her something."

Marguerite sighs and I wish there were something I could say besides 'I'm sorry.'

"She's using money to control us and I fall for it every time," she says. "I'm trying to make peace so that my husband is happy, but it just makes me more angry."

Suddenly, she gets overwhelmed. Her nose turns red and a few tears roll down her cheeks.

I lean over and pull her close to me and wrap my arms around her shoulders as she sobs.

"I'm so sorry." Marguerite tries to push me away, but I just hold her close. "I'm not trying to make any trouble. I'm just pregnant."

"No," I say, pulling her away and looking straight into her eyes. "You have very legitimate concerns and Mom is being awful. She has always used money to manipulate the people around her."

She nods, continuing to sob.

"She loves us on some level, but that doesn't stop her from trying to control us," I say. "She thinks that if she didn't have money, and she didn't have houses, and she didn't have connections, then we wouldn't be there. But what she's really doing is just pushing us away."

"Is it ever going to change?" Marguerite nods.

"One of these days I'm going to reach my breaking point and it's going to be enough."

THE FOLLOWING MORNING, I decide to stop wasting time and call Vasko. He answers on the second ring and I dive right in. I tell him about his financials and the fact that I do not agree with this investment.

He listens carefully and waits. He doesn't try to convince me of anything.

I tell him that the companies look like they are shell companies used to only funnel money from one place to another, and ones that produce nothing.

"So, why are you calling me?" Vasko asks after a long pause. "If everything about this company is so bad and you have no interest in investing, why are we having this conversation?"

What I don't tell him is that I think that Cedar has made some sort of back door deal with him and he thought that he could get it past me, but he can't.

"I don't have a choice. My boss said that we're going to invest, so I'm here to tell you that you're going to get a $5 million infusion of our investors' money."

"Oh, good. Good, good, good," Vasko says quickly.

I can hear him tapping his pen on the table, almost rushing me off the phone.

The fact that he's not more excited about the news just confirms my suspicions.

"What I'm going to tell you now is that you are going to spend every last cent of this money in the legal and appropriate way. Cedar may not take his job very seriously, but I do. The investors depend on my recommendation and I'm going to make sure that the decisions that you make with this money aren't wrong."

32

JACQUELINE

My mom's surgery doesn't go as planned, there are complications, and a lot of blood loss.

Dr. Ellis tells me the news in an overly lit hallway, tilting her head to one side.

"So what's going to happen now? What does this mean?" I ask, burying my hands in my pockets.

"It's a wait and see kind of situation," she says. "We have her sedated, but it's going to take time."

How can this be happening? I shake my head. No, no, no, no, no, this isn't right. I want to stomp my feet, throw a punch, hurt someone, so that someone hurts as much as I do.

Later that afternoon, they show me to her room, machines and plugs are everywhere.

Sedated, asleep, trapped somewhere between here and another world.

I tell her I love her. I tell her that I'm here and I sit in the chair next to the bed for hours until they tell me I can't stay any longer.

Darkness falls. I return to the hotel apartment and look around at my mom's clothes. I was supposed to be here tonight, alone, but tomorrow, or maybe the day after, she was supposed to come back with me.

The surgery was going to make everything better; remove the cancer, extend her life, not make her a vegetable.

Don't think like that, I say to myself over and over again, as I pace around the living room.

My legs start to feel incredibly heavy, impossible to lift. Sitting down on the edge of the bed, I pull them up to my chest and hug myself as tightly as possible.

What am I going to do now? I wonder as my body begins to shake.

My income is running out.

The little bit of savings that I had is practically gone.

I was going to start looking for work after we got back. But staying here longer? That never occurred to either of us. I can't even afford this apartment for another week and our flights back are booked for Friday.

I hate how selfish and narcissistic I am being, thinking about nothing but my own problems.

But the truth is that's what I have to do; not think about the possibility of her not coming out of that sedated state. If I let my mind go there, if I think about even the slightest possibility of her *not* coming back to me, I just don't know what I'll do.

The following day is just like the one before and the one before that. There are updates on oxygen levels.

The pulse ox level is at 87%. Her condition is now considered critical, but stable, but she's still sedated.

I WANT Dante to be in touch, but I don't expect him to be. We texted a lot initially, but I keep waiting for him to leave me hanging, especially after I tell him that the surgery didn't go well.

When I called him that night after I came home alone from the hospital, when I cried and I cried, I knew that I was burning bridges. I was overwhelming him with too much drama and he had every right to never talk to me again.

And then I didn't answer any of his calls the next day. I ignored him for three days.

I pushed him away, and yet he kept coming around.

It's like there was nothing I could do to scare him off, and that's exactly what scared me.

During those first few days of waiting in the hospital room, every minute was like an hour and every hour was like a day.

I sit alone in the hospital room where nothing changes except for the numbers on the monitors that are hooked up to my mom.

But being alone isn't good for me. I reach out to a few friends. The only one that calls back is Allison.

We video chat and I relay all the statistics and the information that I know, and I feel like I'm talking about sports.

"She's going to get better. She's going to get better." Allison keeps promising me.

These are empty promises, just like the ones that I made to myself. But I'll take any prayers, good vibes, and well wishes that I can get at this point.

When the conversation reaches a lull, I ask Allison about her boyfriend. Sitting on the couch, she props her phone up higher on her knee and rolls her eyes.

"What's going on? Did I hit a sore subject?" I ask.

She makes another face.

"Okay, now you have to tell me." I smile.

"No, I'm not going to tell you."

"Come on."

"Well, he doesn't exactly agree with my lifestyle choice, if you want to call it that."

"What's the problem, exactly? Does he want to join you or is he being jealous?"

I like talking about this; it's a nice distraction.

"Well, for one, I don't think he has a say at all since I wouldn't call whatever we have an official relationship."

"I guess…" I force myself to agree.

"I just don't understand why he's so upset about it."

"Which part again?" I lean over closer to the phone, taking a sip of my water. It feels good to talk like this.

"He's jealous, and of course he wants to come."

"And you don't want him to come?" I ask, narrowing my eyes.

"I don't know if I'm ready for that."

I can't help but laugh.

"Look, it's a serious problem," Allison says. "I think I'm going to break up with him. I kind of like this one guy I met at Redemption."

I smile, considering the irony of the situation. "You know, you're not *supposed* to date people you meet there."

"Yeah, it's probably a mistake."

"Tell me that this guy at least doesn't have a…" I'm not sure if I should say girlfriend or wife so I settle on, "partner."

"No, he doesn't." Allison shakes her head. "I'm certain of it."

I have told her a little bit about Dante, but suddenly I'm tempted to tell her more.

"He keeps calling me," I say.

"Is that a bad thing?"

"No, but … I cried so much when I told him about my mom."

"What does that matter?"

"I feel like an idiot. I mean, I literally sobbed into the phone and just told him everything that was going on, and I haven't talked to him since."

"How long has it been?"

"Like three days."

"Oh my God, Jacqueline, c'mon. He clearly likes you. I mean, he's hanging around even though you're acting so ridiculously desperate."

"That's what I'm talking about," I snap at her. "*Why* is he so interested?"

"I was joking, you moron," Allison says, tilting her head to one side and propping it up with her hand. "Look, maybe he actually likes you."

33

JACQUELINE

The following evening, after another day of avoiding taking his calls and just replying casually over text, but saying nothing in particular, I order some food from the Denny's at the corner and take a walk over to Main Street to pick it up.

I window shop, looking into all the little boutiques and even venture in the one that sells cool vintage items found in nice flea markets; artistic glass bowls and unusual clothing that only people in New York City and independent films seem to wear. In the back, I find shelves of novels. Most are paperbacks, but there are a few hard covers as well.

I've always loved the smell of a used bookstore. There's something about the paper that has been touched by hundreds of people before me and the stories that have been loved.

The thing about fiction is that it's not the books that you're forced to read in school that you really make a connection with. It's not the ones that need explanations and analysis, but it's really the ones that you read for pleasure. It's all about the ones that you re-read over and over again, because you happen to love the characters or because the characters on some level, despite all of their obstacles and problems, resemble you.

That's what I've always tried to find in fiction. I've looked for books that were basically about me. I wanted to read about girls who are not particularly confident at first, gaining in that strength and growing into proud, competent women.

"May I help you with anything?" An older woman with bright purple nails and a shaved head walks up to me.

She has a Bruce Springsteen T-shirt on and the kind of fire in her eyes that's difficult to describe.

"No, I'm good. I'm just browsing."

"You're new around here?" she asks.

"I'm not from here."

"Oh, you have a family member in the hospital?"

I nod again, not really wanting to talk about it.

"We have people coming in here trying to pass the time while they wait. How is your family member doing?"

"Not good," I state. "It's kind of a wait and see type of situation."

"Oh, I'm really sorry about that, honey," she says, taking a step forward and draping her arm around me.

Suddenly all of the emotions that I've been bottling up and keeping to myself rush to the surface.

I push myself away and I try to keep the tears from streaming down my face, and when that's not possible, I wipe them as quickly as I can, looking away.

"It's my mom," I whisper.

She gives me a moment, not saying a word.

"You're going to be all right," she says when I look up at her. "It's in God's hands now, whatever happens."

"Yeah, I guess. I just wish that there were something I could do."

"You're thinking about her. You're sending her good vibes, positive energy. That's all you can do, but don't kick yourself over anything. Your mom knows how much you love her and how worried you are."

When the woman walks away, I see the scar on the back of her head going from the nape of her neck, all the way to the top. I want to ask her about it, but I already know as much as I perhaps should. She had some sort of surgery and seems to be in recovery.

Looking through the books again, I choose seven titles that I hope will let me think about something other than my own issues: a few heart-pounding thrillers, two suspense novels about marriage issues and lies and secrets, and a couple of dark romances.

"That will be $7.50," she says, pounding into the ancient cash register.

When a little receipt prints out, she hands it to me. I hand her the cash, and she offers a bag, but I decline. I have a whole stash of them at the hotel that I don't know what to do with.

I walk all the way back to the hotel, enjoying the slightly warmer air. The clouds are hanging low now, filtering the sunset, creating bright yellow and gold hues over the horizon.

I wanted to go see more of this place. It looks beautiful, full of nature and wilderness and people that are a lot nicer than they are back home. But, of course, I can't do that. My life is tied to the hospital now.

Holding onto the books, I reach into my pocket to retrieve the door key. It all becomes rather precarious when the books start to shift. I lift up my foot to try to keep them in place with my knee. Just as I push the door key into the slot and it dings green, the books come tumbling to the floor.

"Shit," I mumble to myself.

"Can I help you with that?"

A familiar voice sends shivers up my spine.

No, it can't be him, I say to myself. No, don't even think that.

I turn around slowly, my eyes going all the way, starting from his gray slim-cut suit. The white button down shirt is tucked into his belt, and he's not wearing a tie.

I'm afraid to meet his eyes. I look at his strong jawline and the slightly parted lips and I know exactly who it is.

"Dante?" I ask. "What are you doing here?"

"I was in town for business, so I thought I would say hi."

He kneels down to pick up my books.

My heart starts to thump out of my chest.

"But why are you here?" I ask him while he holds my book collection in his hands, waiting for me to open the door.

I hesitate.

"Look, if you want me to leave, just tell me. But I was worried about you. I thought that you'd want someone to talk to during this difficult time."

"So, you just showed up?"

He nods. "Was that wrong?"

"I don't know."

I shake my head, blood thumping through my brain, and I can practically hear it slosh around.

"Here, let me just drop these off for you, and I can go."

I open the door, and we walk into the dark one-bedroom apartment hotel with a small college-sized refrigerator in the corner and a small microwave on top.

I flip on the light because the one window with heavy curtains doesn't provide enough of it.

There's a durable but rather uncomfortable couch right near the front door, and I ask him if he wants anything to drink.

"What do you have?" he asks, plopping the books onto the reddish brown wooden table that has been serving as both a dining room and an office. "You've got quite a haul here. Going to be busy."

I nod, walking over to the kitchenette and grabbing two glasses, filling them with water.

"This is all I have." I hand one to him.

"You know, I thought that you'd be more of a Kindle kind of reader."

"I am," I say, shifting my weight from one foot to another, realizing that I'm still wearing my boots and my coat. "I just saw the thrift store and haven't read a paperback in a while."

"Well, they look interesting," Dante says, going through the book covers.

Suddenly, I have a flashback to being a kid.

I used to devour *Sweet Valley High* books, borrowing them from the library. But every time that my dad saw the covers, he just made fun of me, saying that they were stupid, pointless, girly trash.

After that, I would hide them in my backpack. I would always hide them under more important books that were supposedly a better representation of me as a person. But the truth is that he was the one who was an asshole.

There are no right or wrong books; they're just right or wrong novels for you. There are no such things as guilty pleasures; there are just pleasures.

It's okay to like anything you like and no one should tell you otherwise.

The truth is that people who make fun of popular books and the writers who write them are the ones who've never written a book themselves and don't know how hard it is to write one.

I wait for Dante, the serious corporate Master of the Universe type, to tell me that romance novels are stupid. But he surprises me.

"I've read these two and I think you'll like them. They're really good. As far as this one goes, let me know how it is. It seems really hot."

He smiles at the corner of his lips, holding the romance.

"You know, you're full of surprises," I say to him after a long pause.

"I am?" he asks.

"Yeah. I mean, if I hadn't called some *other* guy back a million times, I don't think he'd be sitting here talking to me about books."

"I can leave," Dante says, pointing to the door. "I mean, you pretty much told me to fuck off in not so many words, and maybe I should have listened."

"No, I'd like you to stay. I got some Denny's," I say after thinking about it for a moment.

"I don't want to eat your dinner."

"I got two orders," I say, taking off my jacket and hanging it on the hook near the front door.

"You did?" he asks.

I nod. "I didn't want to order more in a few hours or in the morning when I got hungry, so I figured I'd just get another order and warm it up."

"Well, if you don't mind, I'd love to join you."

Dante takes off his jacket, hanging it next to mine. He slips out of his dress shoes and places them neatly next to my boots.

"Thank you for coming," I say and start to unpack the food.

34

JACQUELINE

Dante and I have a pleasant dinner over eggs, hash browns, and pancakes. The food got cold so I warmed it up in the microwave. It shouldn't taste great, but eating it here with him makes it the most delicious thing in the world.

We talk about nothing and everything. I tell him about Dartmouth and Allison, wanting to be a journalist, and my current status of unemployment and lack of prospects.

He tells me about his overbearing mother and University of Maine, and how much of a disappointment it was that he didn't go to Yale like his brother.

"So did you not think that you were going to get in?" I ask, trying to be as tactful as possible.

"No, I was certain I would."

"Oh, well, isn't that cocky of you." I smile.

He tosses his hair from one side to another.

"No, I'm certain I would get in because my grandfather bought them a building and wrote it into the agreement that the trust would pay for the upkeep in perpetuity as long as all of his descendants get to go there."

"Oh, wow." I raise an eyebrow.

"Yeah, so I didn't even apply."

"Why did you choose Maine?"

"I love it there. It's beautiful, wild. People are not so pretentious."

"I can't imagine that your mom was very pleased with that decision," I say, slathering my pancake in a generous amount of maple syrup.

"No, she wasn't, but we go through these hot and cold periods where we talk, don't talk. She's not the easiest person to have a relationship with."

When I find out that Dante got sent to boarding school at age seven, my heart goes out to him. He doesn't shy away from telling me how much he was hurt and how scared he was, and I immediately realize that he's a lot different from any other man than I have ever met.

We talk late into the night and we laugh. We talk about our favorite movies and books and shows, and we fall asleep a few times on top of the sheets.

The second time I doze off, I rouse a few minutes later and I see Dante deep asleep. His face is relaxed, eyes closed, body limp, and I watch him sleep for a little bit and wonder why he's suddenly in my life.

I've put up so many guardrails and so many obstacles, and now I wonder if maybe I did that just so that I could find him. His starched white shirt is now hopelessly wrinkled, and he lies on his side, propping his head up with his elbow, using it like a pillow.

My mouth feels parched, so I sit up on my side of the bed. I pour myself a glass of water very quietly from the tap, not wanting to make much noise.

Instead of being exhausted, I am energized. I pick up a book, the first one on top, the dark romantic suspense set in a house in the woods. I begin to read. Two chapters in, and I'm pretty certain I won't be able to sleep, but then the next thing I know is that I open my eyes and it's morning. The shades are still drawn, but a little bit of bright sunshine is peeking in from underneath.

Dante's sitting at the table in the corner, typing quietly into his laptop, the blue screen illuminating his face.

"Oh, I'm sorry. Did I wake you?" he asks.

I shake my head no. The book lies open flat with the spine bent next to me.

"Saw that you made quite a dent into that one. What do you think?"

"It was so scary at first. I wasn't sure if I'd be able to get through it," I say, stretching my arms as I sit up in bed.

"Thanks for letting me stay over." He smiles.

"Sure." I nod.

I look at the time. In another hour, I can go see my mom.

"Last night was really nice," I say, walking over to him.

He grabs my hand and pulls me closer for a kiss, but I push him away. "No, I can't."

"Oh, I'm sorry. I misread things," he says.

I laugh. "No, I'm just ... I haven't brushed my teeth yet."

He smiles, grabs my hand, and presses his lips to

mine. I don't want to open my mouth, but my body seems to take over.

His hand snakes its way underneath my T-shirt, and my nipples immediately get hard to the touch.

Suddenly, my desperate need for a shower doesn't seem to matter anymore.

Dante kisses me harder and harder. His hands pull me closer to him. He tugs on my hair just slightly.

My whole body explodes in anticipation.

I'm dressed in a ratty T-shirt and a loose pair of pajama bottoms that somehow fall off of me with one quick tug.

He grabs my butt cheeks, squeezing tightly. I reach for his crumpled shirt and I struggle with the buttons, running my fingers up and down his hard stomach. I feel each one of the muscles flex, his tan olive skin in stark contrast to my own.

He lowers me onto the bed and pulls down my panties, tossing them onto the floor. He makes his way up my inner thighs, and I open my legs for him, arch my back, and close my eyes.

He rubs me a little, kissing just around my thighs and my belly button, but not quite going all the way. When I've had enough of the teasing, I reach down and grab onto his large cock, rubbing it hard in my hands.

He moans a little in my ear and helps me push down his pants and his boxer briefs. When our bodies are pressed to one another, he kisses me again and again.

This feels different from how it felt at the club. There was all that mystery and uncertainty, but this feels good and comfortable in the best sense.

"Do you have anything?" I whisper into his ear.

"Yeah, in my bag."

He reaches over the bed and grabs it off the side of the chair. I continue to kiss him, licking his abs and then going further and further south, grabbing his butt cheeks with my hands, and then my phone goes off.

I usually keep the sound off, but the hospital told me that they will get in touch in case of any emergency. Grabbing it off the nightstand, I answer immediately.

"Your mother's condition is getting worse. We'd like you to come in," the nurse says on the other end.

Her voice is professional and courteous and sounds like the kiss of death.

35

JACQUELINE

W hen we get to the hospital, Dante holds my hand as Dr. Ellis meets with us in front of my mom's room.

"The pneumonia has become quite severe," she says. "She will need to show a positive change within the first two weeks, otherwise there'll be nothing that we can do for her."

My heart sinks, but Dante pulses his hand to show his support.

"We just turned her on her stomach, oxygen saturation is just at 87, but that was just when she was turned," Dr. Ellis continues to rattle off information that I can barely process let alone understand. "She still has to get into the flow of being turned onto her stomach. She needed a little bit more sedation during turning, but there has been no growth seen in the blood cultures. Our goal is to try to manage to get her blood sugar to a healthier level. In this past week as you know, she needed a lot of extra sedation medication, but luckily, none this morning."

"So why did you call me now?" I ask.

"She had a scary setback just an hour ago with the pulse ox dropping dangerously low when we went to turn her on her back. We need to see this aggressive viral form of pneumonia start clearing out of her lungs, to see a more positive sign of her being able to get through this. When we called, things were looking grim. I thought that maybe we would lose her, but she's stable now, still critical, of course."

"No, thank you for calling me," I say. "I needed to be here."

"Visiting hours aren't officially open, but of course you can stay. I'm sorry to have you worry, but ..."

"No, I need all the updates. Please, whenever, it doesn't matter what time of day or night."

"Of course."

After Dr. Ellis leaves, I take a few steps away and I lean against the wall and stare out at the exit sign in the distance, the harsh fluorescent lights blinding me just a little bit until my eyes adjust.

"I'm really sorry, Jacqueline," Dante says.

I see him holding my hand as I dissociate from my body. Our fingers are intertwined but not really. My hand belongs to someone else.

I'm glad that he doesn't say that she's going to be okay or make more promises that he cannot keep. I'm also glad that he's here.

Some time passes and I find myself in front of a vending machine. Dante is there. He asks me what I want, but I can't choose.

I don't want anything, and I can't imagine what any of the stuff inside tastes like.

I just stare at him and wait for him to make the decision: pretzels, and M&M's, and Lay's potato chips. There's another machine with healthier options right next to this one with apples, yogurts, and bananas in various slots.

Without me having to ask, Dante walks over and buys a Granny Smith, handing it to me.

"Do you want this instead?" he asks.

My mouth starts to water and I nod. He wipes the apple on his shirt. When I bite into it, the juices flow, overwhelming my senses.

For a second I feel just a tiny bit better and

that's enough for now. We spend the whole day in the hospital, followed by another.

He's there when I get the updates and he celebrates the little victories, the pulse ox staying stable at 90, dipping down to 89 and then going back up to 91 once in a while.

I hold her hand.

I tell Mom how much I love her and how much I want her to come back to me. The nurses check on her every hour. The last two times, they don't have any problems turning her back onto her stomach with the stats remaining good, pulse ox stable at 90.

They take her off the machine. The FIO2 is at 80%, but that's just helping to give her the extra oxygen that she needs right now. Her blood sugar has come down to the mid hundreds and I feel a small relief about the stability of her condition.

Right now it looks like she might make it, but there's still a long way to go. A whole field of mines to avoid.

And through it all, Dante stays. He cancels a work trip and he puts in a lot of hours on his laptop, sneaking it in whenever I'm resting or watching Netflix or reading.

The days all blend into one and Friday comes sooner than I think it will.

"Shit," I mumble to myself.

"What? What's wrong?"

"I forgot I have to pay," I say when I see the note on the door of the hotel room.

We walk over to the office where a dissatisfied older gentleman with a TV blaring in the background tells me that I owe another $400 if I want to extend my stay.

I hesitate.

I know that one of my credit cards is overdrawn and I don't have the cash for this.

Dante pulls me aside and asks, "Do you want to stay in a more comfortable place?"

I shrug. "I don't know. I mean, this place is fine."

"I'm going to cover it."

"No, I can't ask you to do that." I shake my head.

"Don't worry about it. My only request is can we stay in a little bit of a nicer spot?"

Mom's condition seems to stabilize. The next day, there is no news. Just updates about higher than normal oxygen levels and a normal blood pressure.

Dr. Ellis mentions that she's hopeful, and Dante takes me out to celebrate. He ended up booking a suite at the Marriott and with its floor-to-ceiling windows, a view of the pool and the hot tub, as well as the outdoor bar, it's quite an upgrade.

One morning, I wake up early. I leave Dante in the bedroom and decide to do a little yoga following a YouTube routine.

I haven't stretched out or done much in terms of exercise in a while and it feels good to engage my body.

But I had forgotten to charge my computer and, when I try to put it in the middle of the floor, the plug doesn't reach. I see Dante's laptop on the dining room table. I know the code from last night when he was busy chopping up vegetables and asked me to check his email.

When I log in, the windows that were open before pop up. I'm about to close them when I see my mother's name in the subject line.

My mouth drops open.

Dear Mr. Dante Langston,

Thank you for paying for Elizabeth Archer's treatment.

Unfortunately, the payment you submitted was for the surgery only.

If you're unable or unwilling to pay for the rest of the treatment, we will have to be in touch with the patient's next of kin in order to make the proper arrangements.

I stare at the screen, reading the email over and over again, trying to understand how and why he is involved with any of this.

———

THANK you for reading DARK INTENTIONS! I hope you enjoyed Jacqueline and Dante's love story. Their story continues with **DARK REDEMPTION**...

He saved my mother's life. Now, I owe him a debt. But I don't even know who he is.

Dante Langston is man of extreme wealth and privilege and just as much darkness.

What I don't yet know is that he already knows me.

He has been watching and waiting. He needs to stay away to protect his secrets but he can't.

What happens when I find out the debt I owe is to *him*?

What happens when I find out the other secrets that he is much more desperate to keep?

ONE CLICK DARK REDEMPTION NOW >

Cᴀɴ'ᴛ ɢᴇᴛ ᴇɴᴏᴜɢʜ of Jacqueline and Dante?
Grab the FREE BONUS scene now!

Grab the FREE BONUS scene now!

Sɪɢɴ up for my **newsletter** to find out when I have new books!

You can also join my Facebook group, **Charlotte Byrd's Reader Club**, for exclusive giveaways and sneak peaks of future books.

I appreciate you sharing my books and telling your friends about them. Reviews help readers find my books! Please leave a review on your favorite site.

I AM THRILLED to offer a sneak peak of **BLACK EDGE**, a bestselling full-length dark contemporary novel about a secret auction and the lengths that people are willing to go for love....

"HERE IT IS! HERE IT IS!" my roommate Caroline yells at the top of her lungs as she runs into my room.

We were friends all through Yale and we moved to New York together after graduation.

Even though I've known Caroline for what feels like a million years, I am still shocked by the exuberance of her voice. It's quite loud given the smallness of her body.

Caroline is one of those super skinny girls who can eat pretty much anything without gaining a pound.

Unfortunately, I am not that talented. In fact, my body seems to have the opposite gift. I can eat nothing but vegetables for a week straight, eat one slice of pizza, and gain a pound.

"What is it?" I ask, forcing myself to sit up.

It's noon and I'm still in bed.

My mother thinks I'm depressed and wants me to see her shrink.

She might be right, but I can't fathom the strength.

"The invitation!" Caroline says jumping in bed next to me.

I stare at her blankly.

And then suddenly it hits me.

This must be *the* invitation.

"You mean…it's…"

"Yes!" she screams and hugs me with excitement.

"Oh my God!" She gasps for air and pulls away from me almost as quickly.

"Hey, you know I didn't brush my teeth yet," I say turning my face away from hers.

"Well, what are you waiting for? Go brush them," she instructs.

Begrudgingly, I make my way to the bathroom.

We have been waiting for this invitation for some time now.

And by we, I mean Caroline.

I've just been playing along, pretending to care, not really expecting it to show up.

Without being able to contain her excitement, Caroline bursts through the door when my mouth is still full of toothpaste.

She's jumping up and down, holding a box in her hand.

"Wait, what's that?" I mumble and wash my mouth out with water.

"This is it!" Caroline screeches and pulls me into the living room before I have a chance to wipe my mouth with a towel.

"But it's a box," I say staring at her.

"Okay, okay," Caroline takes a couple of deep yoga breaths, exhaling loudly.

She puts the box carefully on our dining room table. There's no address on it.

It looks something like a fancy gift box with a big monogrammed C in the middle.

Is the C for Caroline?

"Is this how it came? There's no address on it?" I ask.

"It was hand-delivered," Caroline whispers.

I hold my breath as she carefully removes the top part, revealing the satin and silk covered wood box inside.

The top of it is gold plated with whimsical twirls all around the edges, and the mirrored area is engraved with her full name.

Caroline Elizabeth Kennedy Spruce.

Underneath her name is a date, one week in the future. 8 PM.

We stare at it for a few moments until Caroline reaches for the elegant knob to open the box.

Inside, Caroline finds a custom monogram made of foil in gold on silk emblazoned on the inside of the flap cover.

There's also a folio covered in silk. Caroline carefully opens the folio and finds another foil monogram and the invitation.

The inside invitation is one layer, shimmer white, with gold writing.

"Is this for real? How many layers of invitation are there?" I ask.

But the presentation is definitely doing its job. We are both duly impressed.

"There's another knob," I say, pointing to the knob in front of the box.

I'm not sure how we had missed it before.

Caroline carefully pulls on this knob, revealing a drawer that holds the inserts (a card with directions and a response card).

"Oh my God, I can't go to this alone," Caroline mumbles, turning to me.

I stare blankly at her.

Getting invited to this party has been her dream ever since she found out about it from someone in the Cicada 17, a super-secret society at Yale.

"Look, here, it says that I can bring a friend," she yells out even though I'm standing right next to her.

"It probably says a date. A plus one?" I say.

"No, a friend. Girl preferred," Caroline reads off the invitation card.

That part of the invitation is in very small ink, as if someone made the person stick it on, without their express permission.

"I don't want to crash," I say.

Frankly, I don't really want to go.

These kind of upper-class events always make me feel a little bit uncomfortable.

"Hey, aren't you supposed to be at work?" I ask.

"Eh, I took a day off," Caroline says waving her arm. "I knew that the invitation would come today and I just couldn't deal with work. You know how it is."

I nod. Sort of.

Caroline and I seem like we come from the same world.

We both graduated from private school, we both went to Yale, and our parents belong to the same exclusive country club in Greenwich, Connecticut.

But we're not really that alike.

Caroline's family has had money for many generations going back to the railroads.

My parents were an average middle class family from Connecticut.

They were both teachers and our idea of summering was renting a 1-bedroom bungalow near Clearwater, FL for a week.

But then my parents got divorced when I was 8, and my mother started tutoring kids to make extra money.

The pay was the best in Greenwich, where parents paid more than $100 an hour.

And that's how she met, Mitch Willoughby, my stepfather.

He was a widower with a five-year old daughter who was not doing well after her mom's untimely death.

Even though Mom didn't usually tutor anyone younger than 12, she agreed to take a meeting with

Mitch and his daughter because $200 an hour was too much to turn down.

Three months later, they were in love and six months later, he asked her to marry him on top of the Eiffel Tower.

They got married, when I was 11, in a huge 450-person ceremony in Nantucket.

So even though Caroline and I run in the same circles, we're not really from the same circle.

It has nothing to do with her, she's totally accepting, it's me.

I don't always feel like I belong.

Caroline majored in art-history at Yale, and she now works at an exclusive contemporary art gallery in Soho.

It's chic and tiny, featuring only 3 pieces of art at a time.

Ash, the owner - I'm not sure if that's her first or last name - mainly keeps the space as a showcase. What the gallery really specializes in is going to wealthy people's homes and choosing their art for them.

They're basically interior designers, but only for art.

None of the pieces sell for anything less than

$200 grand, but Caroline's take home salary is about $21,000.

Clearly, not enough to pay for our 2 bedroom apartment in Chelsea.

Her parents cover her part of the rent and pay all of her other expenses.

Mine do too, of course.

Well, Mitch does.

I only make about $27,000 at my writer's assistant job and that's obviously not covering my half of our $6,000 per month apartment.

So, what's the difference between me and Caroline?

I guess the only difference is that I feel bad about taking the money.

I have a $150,000 school loan from Yale that I don't want Mitch to pay for.

It's my loan and I'm going to pay for it myself, dammit.

Plus, unlike Caroline, I know that real people don't really live like this.

Real people like my dad, who is being pressured to sell the house for more than a million dollars that he and my mom bought back in the late 80's (the neighborhood has gone up in price and teachers now have to make way for tech entrepreneurs and real estate moguls).

"How can you just not go to work like that? Didn't you use all of your sick days flying to Costa Rica last month?" I ask.

"Eh, who cares? Ash totally understands. Besides, she totally owes me. If it weren't for me, she would've never closed that geek millionaire who had the hots for me and ended up buying close to a million dollars' worth of art for his new mansion."

Caroline does have a way with men.

She's fun and outgoing and perky.

The trick, she once told me, is to figure out exactly what the guy wants to hear.

Because a geek millionaire, as she calls anyone who has made money in tech, does not want to hear the same thing that a football player wants to hear.

And neither of them want to hear what a trust fund playboy wants to hear.

But Caroline isn't a gold digger.

Not at all.

Her family owns half the East Coast.

And when it comes to men, she just likes to have fun.

I look at the time.

It's my day off, but that doesn't mean that I

want to spend it in bed in my pajamas, listening to Caroline obsessing over what she's going to wear.

No, today, is my day to actually get some writing done.

I'm going to Starbucks, getting a table in the back, near the bathroom, and am actually going to finish this short story that I've been working on for a month.

Or maybe start a new one.

I go to my room and start getting dressed.

I have to wear something comfortable, but something that's not exactly work clothes.

I hate how all of my clothes have suddenly become work clothes. It's like they've been tainted.

They remind me of work and I can't wear them out anymore on any other occasion. I'm not a big fan of my work, if you can't tell.

Caroline follows me into my room and plops down on my bed.

I take off my pajamas and pull on a pair of leggings.

Ever since these have become the trend, I find myself struggling to force myself into a pair of jeans.

They're just so comfortable!

"Okay, I've come to a decision," Caroline says. "You *have* to come with me!"

"Oh, I have to come with you?" I ask, incredulously. "Yeah, no, I don't think so."

"Oh c'mon! Please! Pretty please! It will be so much fun!"

"Actually, you can't make any of those promises. You have no idea what it will be," I say, putting on a long sleeve shirt and a sweater with a zipper in the front.

Layers are important during this time of year.

The leaves are changing colors, winds are picking up, and you never know if it's going to be one of those gorgeous warm, crisp New York days they like to feature in all those romantic comedies or a soggy, overcast dreary day that only shows up in one scene at the end when the two main characters fight or break up (but before they get back together again).

"Okay, yes, I see your point," Caroline says, sitting up and crossing her legs. "But here is what we *do* know. We do know that it's going to be amazing. I mean, look at the invitation. It's a freakin' box with engravings and everything!"

Usually, Caroline is much more eloquent and better at expressing herself.

"Okay, yes, the invitation is impressive," I admit.

"And as you know, the invitation is everything. I mean, it really sets the mood for the party. The event! And not just the mood. It establishes a certain expectation. And this box…"

"Yes, the invitation definitely sets up a certain expectation," I agree.

"So?"

"So?" I ask her back.

"Don't you want to find out what that expectation is?"

"No." I shake my head categorically.

"Okay. So what else do we know?" Caroline asks rhetorically as I pack away my Mac into my bag.

"I have to go, Caroline," I say.

"No, listen. The yacht. Of course, the yacht. How could I bury the lead like that?" She jumps up and down with excitement again.

"We also know that it's going to be this super exclusive event on a *yacht*! And not just some small 100 footer, but a *mega*-yacht."

I stare at her blankly, pretending to not be impressed.

When Caroline first found out about this party,

through her ex-boyfriend, we spent days trying to figure out what made this event so special.

But given that neither of us have been on a yacht before, at least not a mega-yacht – we couldn't quite get it.

"You know the yacht is going to be amazing!"

"Yes, of course," I give in. "But that's why I'm sure that you're going to have a wonderful time by yourself. I have to go."

I grab my keys and toss them into the bag.

"Ellie," Caroline says.

The tone of her voice suddenly gets very serious, to match the grave expression on her face.

"Ellie, please. I don't think I can go by myself."

Want to read more? **One Click BLACK EDGE now!**

CONNECT WITH CHARLOTTE BYRD

Sign up for my **newsletter** to find out when I have new books!

You can also join my Facebook group, **Charlotte Byrd's Reader Club**, for exclusive giveaways and sneak peaks of future books.

I appreciate you sharing my books and telling your friends about them. Reviews help readers find my books! Please leave a review on your favorite site.

Sign up for my newsletter: https://www. subscribepage.com/byrdVIPList

Join my Facebook Group: https://www.facebook. com/groups/276340079439433/

Bonus Points: Follow me on BookBub and Goodreads!

ABOUT CHARLOTTE BYRD

Charlotte Byrd is the bestselling author of romantic suspense novels. She has sold over 1 Million books and has been translated into five languages.

She lives near Palm Springs, California with her husband, son, a toy Australian Shepherd and a Ragdoll cat. Charlotte is addicted to books and Netflix and she loves hot weather and crystal blue water.

Write her here:

charlotte@charlotte-byrd.com

Check out her books here:

www.charlotte-byrd.com

Connect with her here:

www.facebook.com/charlottebyrdbooks

www.instagram.com/charlottebyrdbooks

www.twitter.com/byrdauthor

Want to hear about new releases, free books and get exclusive giveaways?

Sign up for my newsletter!

Sign up for my newsletter: https://www.
subscribepage.com/byrdVIPList

Join my Facebook Group: https://www.facebook.
com/groups/276340079439433/

Bonus Points: Follow me on BookBub and
Goodreads!

amazon.com/Charlotte-Byrd/e/B013MN45Q6

facebook.com/charlottebyrdbooks

bookbub.com/profile/charlotte-byrd

twitter.com/byrdauthor

instagram.com/charlottebyrdbooks

ALSO BY CHARLOTTE BYRD

All books are available at ALL major retailers! If you can't find it, please email me at charlotte@charlotte-byrd.com

Dark Intentions Series
Dark Intentions
Dark Redemption
Dark Sins

The Perfect Stranger Series
The Perfect Stranger
The Perfect Cover
The Perfect Lie
The Perfect Life
The Perfect Getaway

All the Lies Series
All the Lies
All the Secrets
All the Doubts

Tell me Series
Tell Me to Stop
Tell Me to Go
Tell Me to Stay
Tell Me to Run
Tell Me to Fight
Tell Me to Lie

Wedlocked Trilogy
Dangerous Engagement
Lethal Wedding
Fatal Wedding

Tangled Series
Tangled up in Ice
Tangled up in Pain
Tangled up in Lace
Tangled up in Hate
Tangled up in Love

Black Series

Made in the USA
Middletown, DE
20 April 2023

29202535R00194